PRAISE FOR THE TALES OF TERROR COLLECTION

Tales of Terror from the Tunnel's Mouth

'Genuinely, thrillingly horrible.
And I mean that in a good way'
Independent

'Inventive, deadpan, sardonic and cruel . . .
a creepy autumnal treat'
Financial Times

'Spine-chilling thrillers . . . a wonderfully
nightmarish journey of the imagination'
Daily Mail

'A classic in the making'
Independent on Sunday

Tales of Terror from the Black Ship

'Wonderfully macabre and beautifully
crafted horror stories'
Chris Riddell

'A fantastic page-turner, with a really scary ending'
Independent on Sunday

TALES OF TERROR FROM THE TUNNEL'S MOUTH

CHRIS PRIESTLEY

BLOOMSBURY

LONDON BERLIN NEW YORK SYDNEY

Bloomsbury Publishing, London, Berlin, New York and Sydney

First published in Great Britain in 2009 by Bloomsbury Publishing Plc
36 Soho Square, London, W1D 3QY

This paperback edition published in March 2011

A CIP catalogue record of this book is available from the British Library

ISBN 978 1 4088 0274 8

FSC
www.fsc.org
MIX
Paper from
responsible sources
FSC® C018072

Typeset by Dorchester Typesetting Group Ltd
Printed in Great Britain by Clays Ltd, St Ives Plc

1 3 5 7 9 10 8 6 4 2

www.talesofterror.co.uk
www.bloomsbury.com

For H.S. with thanks

CONTENTS

1

THE TRAIN

It was the first railway journey I had ever made alone. My stepmother had come to the station to see me off and proceeded to embarrass me with unwanted hugs and kisses and the nursery voice she always adopted for such displays of affection.

My father was away at war, fighting the Boers in the searing heat of South Africa, and I would gladly have joined him there in preference to spending another moment with his dreary and irritating wife. Not that I'd ever had what you might call a close relationship with my father either.

But to my relief, the holidays had finally come to

an end and I was off to a new school. Ordinarily I would, no doubt, have felt nervous about this move, but life with my stepmother over those weeks had been an ordeal that had tested and emboldened me to face anything my new school might present by way of challenges. I was fearless.

Or so I thought.

We had been waiting on the platform for the better part of half an hour, my stepmother having insisted on us being preposterously early, so concerned was she that I might miss my train.

We were sitting on a wooden bench on the platform and, conversation having long ago run dry, I was reading the London Illustrated News and my stepmother was dozing. She has the most extraordinary capacity for falling asleep at a moment's notice. Any kind of pause in the routine was an excuse for a nap. I swear she was more cat than human.

I looked about me. It was a dull, rural English station on a rather pleasant and sunny morning. There were three or four other passengers who had arrived during the time we were there, and there was a portly, bearded stationmaster, who walked up and down the platform, looking at his watch every two minutes and smiling and tipping his hat to everyone he passed.

All was, in fact, utterly mundane, drearily peaceful – until, that is, my stepmother awoke from her catnap with a sudden strangled yelp that made me jump several inches in the air and caused concerned and embarrassed glances from the other passengers waiting at the station.

'For goodness' sake,' I said, blushing and trying not to catch the eye of any of the onlookers. 'There are people watching.'

'Oh!' she said, turning to me in a quite delirious way, her eyes wild. 'But I've had the most awful premonition.'

I should mention at this point that my stepmother considered herself to have a gift in that regard.

'You were dreaming,' I said, smiling at a man who was looking at my stepmother with an expression that betrayed a not unreasonable concern that she may have escaped from a lunatic asylum.

'But I had the distinct impression of danger, my dear: deadly danger,' she said, still staring at me in that deranged manner.

'What on earth are you talking about, madam?' I hissed.

'I wish you wouldn't call me that,' she said, putting her hands to her temples.

I was fully aware that she did not like it, but there was no way on this earth that I was going to call her 'Mother', as I knew she wanted me to.

'What danger?' I asked again.

'I do not know,' she said. 'I see . . . I see a kiss.'

'A kiss?' I said with a laugh. 'It doesn't sound dangerous. Or at least not deadly dangerous. Unless I am kissing a crocodile.'

'A kiss,' she repeated. 'And a tunnel – a long, dark and awful tunnel . . .'

'I am to kiss a tunnel? Well, that at least sounds a little dangerous,' I said with a withering smile.

But my stepmother continued to stare at me in the oddest way and, ridiculous though her statement was, there was something unnerving about her gaze, and I was forced to look away.

This 'premonition' of my stepmother's was as vague as usual. I sighed and looked down the line, willing the train to arrive. I longed with all my heart to be away from her.

'You were sleeping and had a nightmare,' I said, making no effort to disguise my disdain. 'Or a *day*mare – or whatever it is one has when one is dozing on a station platform in broad daylight.'

My stepmother bristled at my tone of voice.

'Please do not talk to me in that way,' she said.

4

'I'm sorry if I've said anything to offend you,' I answered, looking away.

But I was not sorry at all.

A whistle sounded down the track and heralded the imminent arrival of my train. I could not have been more relieved. I stood up.

'Well,' I said. 'Here it is.'

'My dear boy.' My stepmother flung herself upon me in the most vulgar fashion.

'Please,' I said, squirming with embarrassment. 'There are people watching.'

I finally extricated myself from her jellyfish embrace and, picking up my bag, I moved to board the carriage.

'I do wish you would catch another train,' she said, grabbing me by the sleeve.

I carried on regardless.

'After waiting here for the best part of an hour? I don't think so.'

The idea that I would willingly spend another moment on that platform with her! I stepped up into the carriage and slammed the door shut with a force I hoped might transmit some of my feelings, but when I looked through the open window of the carriage door, my stepmother was holding a handkerchief to her face and making fanning motions with her other hand, as if she were about to swoon (while surreptitiously glancing about in the hope of an audience, of course).

A burst of steam hid her from view and I found the illusion of her disappearance intensely pleasurable, but as the train moved off I caught a glimpse of her frantically waving. I pretended not to see and set about finding a seat.

I walked down the corridor, looking into the compartments until I found one with a vacant window seat. The only other occupant was a stiff, military-looking gentleman with a ruddy face, firm and jutting jaw and exuberant moustache. I will call him the Major. He nodded a greeting as I walked in.

'Would you mind awfully if I joined you, sir?' I asked.

'Not at all,' he said, sitting up to attention at my approach.

I smiled and thanked him, putting my bag in the luggage rack above my seat. The Major sniffed loudly.

'Providing that you are not a whistler,' he continued as I sat down.

'I beg your pardon, sir?'

'A whistler,' he repeated. 'Can't abide a whistler.

Sets my teeth on edge, don't you know.'

'No, sir,' I assured him. 'I am not a whistler.'

'I'm pleased to hear it,' he said with another sniff. 'So many young people are.'

'Not I, sir,' I said.

'Splendid.'

I smiled and looked out of the window, hoping that this might bring an end to the strange conversation, which it thankfully did. The Major picked up the copy of *The Times* he had folded in his lap and began to read, making the odd tut or sniff as he did so.

The train moved on, stopping intermittently at stations as prim and as dull as the one at which I had boarded. At each of these, the carriage gained a new occupant.

The first to join the Major and I, choosing to sit beside me, was a bishop (or so I shall call him): a stout, round-faced man of the cloth who, after wishing us good day, took a pile of handwritten papers from his briefcase and began to study them, occasionally making notes with a fountain pen.

The second passenger to join us was a short and wiry man, whom I decided was a farmer. He sat opposite the Bishop and next to the Major. We all nodded greetings to one another as he sat down.

The Farmer's hands had clearly known hard work and his shoes had not been cleaned quite thoroughly enough and still bore signs of fresh mud.

At the next station, a tall, cadaverous man entered our compartment. He was on nodding acquaintance with the Major. He had long, pale fingers and a face to match. He was well dressed and carried a copy of the *Lancet*: a surgeon on his way to Harley Street, I had no doubt. He sat next to the Bishop and opposite the Major. The seat opposite me – the other window seat – remained empty.

I suddenly began to feel a little weary. Perhaps the excitement of travelling alone had exhausted me, or perhaps it was the attentions of the warm sunshine through the carriage window. I closed my eyes.

When I opened them again, I realised that, though I was sure I had closed them for but a short moment, I must have been asleep for some time, because the vacant seat in front of me was now occupied by a woman, a rather attractive woman, in a severe kind of way.

She was still young – not so many years older than I – and very pale and slim. Her face was long, her cheekbones high. Her hair was red. Her clothes, from her shoes to her hat, were white.

I smiled and nodded and she smiled back, her pale green eyes staring at me with unnerving intensity.

I nodded again and looked away at the other occupants of our carriage, who were all, every one of them, sound asleep, the Major, ironically, whistling each time he breathed out.

The other difference of note was that the train had come to a halt, despite there being no station in sight. Flattening my face against the window, I could see that the engine had stopped just in front of the mouth of a tunnel and the carriages were at the base of a huge, steep cutting, the banks so high they all but blocked out the sky and left us in a strange twilight.

My stepmother's foolish outburst came back to me and I shook my head. How she would have enjoyed saying, 'I told you so.' But, however irritating an unscheduled stop undoubtedly was, it hardly constituted any kind of danger.

The woman opposite continued to stare and smile at me in such a forward manner that I began to blush a little.

'Where are we, miss?' I said. 'Do you know? Has there been an announcement?'

'You were hoping for an announcement?' she said.

'Yes,' I answered, 'from the guard, telling us where we are and how long the delay might be.'

'Ah,' she said. 'No, I'm afraid there has been no announcement.'

She looked at a gold pocket watch, then at me, then again at the watch before putting it back in the small handbag she held between her long white-gloved fingers on her lap. I looked at my watch too and sighed, giving it a shake.

'What is the time please, miss?' I asked. 'My watch seems to have stopped.'

'The time?' She cocked her head as though she were a small bird. 'Are you in a hurry? The young are always in such a hurry.'

I found this use of the word 'young' a little amusing coming from one who, as I have said, could hardly have been more than ten years older than myself at most. But I let it pass.

'I'm not in a particular hurry,' I replied. 'I'm being met by someone at King's Cross Station and I should not like to keep them waiting. I merely wondered how long we had been standing here.'

'Not long,' she said.

Again I waited in the hope that she might elaborate, but she said nothing further.

'Robert Harper,' I said, holding out my hand as

I thought my father might have done in these circumstances.

'I'm very pleased to meet you, Robert,' she said, taking my hand in hers and holding on to it for longer than I found comfortable. Her grip was surprisingly firm.

She did not, however, give me her name and, though it probably sounds rather weak, I didn't have sufficient confidence to press her for it. I looked out of the window again and sighed in frustration at the continued lack of movement.

'You seem restless, Robert,' said the Woman in White – I refer to her thus in light-hearted reference to Mr Collins' novel of the same name – and I was already regretting giving up my name, as it seemed immediately to give her an advantage over me.

'I am simply impatient to be moving again, Miss . . .' I left a large space hanging for her to offer her name, raising my eyebrows in encouragement, but again she made no move to supply it. I was bold enough to frown, not caring in the least whether she took offence. But if anything her smile widened. I felt sure she was mocking me.

I looked out of the window once more but there was nothing to see, not even the smallest movement of even the smallest creature. As I was thus engaged, a curious illusion made me think that the Woman in White was lurching towards me. I caught sight of her reflection in the window, her face somewhat distorted as she lunged forward. I spun round, pressing myself back into the seat. But I now saw that the Woman in White was sitting unchanged and smiling, and I felt more than a little foolish.

'Is everything all right, Robert?' she asked, not unreasonably.

'I am quite well, thank you,' I said with as much nonchalance as I could muster. 'If a trifle bored.'

The Woman in White nodded sagely and then, with alarming suddenness, clapped her delicate hands together. I was amazed to see that none of the sleepers in our carriage started at the sound.

'We should think of some diversion to amuse ourselves,' she announced.

'Oh?' I said, wondering what she meant.

'You might perhaps enjoy hearing a story,' she said.

'A story?' I asked, a little incredulously. 'Are you a schoolteacher then, miss?' Though as soon as I had asked this, I sensed there was something about her that made this unlikely.

'No,' she said. 'Bless you, I am not a school-teacher.' She smiled to herself, seeming to find the notion privately amusing. 'I assume you ask because you feel that stories are for children?'

'No,' I answered. 'Not at all, miss. I am very fond of stories.'

'And what sort of stories are you fond of, Robert?' she asked with another bird-like cock of the head.

'Well, I don't know,' I said. 'I subscribe to the *Strand Magazine* and there are lots of exciting stories there – like those of Mr Wells. Or the adventures of Sherlock Holmes.'

The Woman in White smiled at me, but as she made no response I felt the need to continue.

'I read Mr Stoker's *Dracula* and thought it frightfully good. Oh – and I think Mr Stevenson a fine writer, too, but that maybe because we have the same name.'

She raised her eyebrows.

'Robert,' I said to clarify. 'We are both called Robert. As in Robert Louis Stevenson?'

'Yes,' she said. 'I realised that.'

'Oh,' I said. 'Sorry.'

Again there was a pause in which I expected the Woman in White to pass some comment on my choice of reading matter, but none came.

13

I thoroughly enjoyed *The Strange Case of Dr Jekyll and Mr Hyde*,' I continued. She smiled and nodded. 'And I thought *The Picture of Dorian Gray* was very good,' I added, hoping that I might shock her by admitting to my enjoyment of such a notorious work. But her face remained impassive.

'It sounds as if you have a taste for stories of unnatural dangers,' she said, 'for works of a supernatural and uncanny bent.'

'I suppose I do,' I admitted, not sure whether she intended this as a criticism or not.

'Well, then,' said the Woman in White. 'I wonder if I might not be able to come up with a story or two to your taste.'

'Are you perhaps a writer yourself, miss?' I asked. I had never actually read anything by a female writer, but I knew they existed. This might explain her peculiar manner. Writers were a strange sort; I knew that much from the newspapers.

She seemed even more amused by this notion than by that of being a schoolteacher.

'No, no. I am not a writer. But I do know a lot of stories.' She tapped the tips of her fingers together and her eyes twinkled. 'Why not let me tell you one, and see if it amuses you?'

I confess I was unenthusiastic, but it would have

been rude to actually refuse. It was a rather eccentric suggestion. I looked concernedly towards our fellow passengers, but they were all still sound asleep.

'It might while away a few minutes,' she said.

'Very well, then,' I said with a sigh and another sideways glance at the other occupants of the carriage, willing at least one of them to wake and rescue me. 'What is the story about?'

'I'm afraid I cannot say much about it without spoiling it for you.'

'Oh,' I said with a nod, and looked out of the window.

'Do you have an interest in botany?' she asked.

'Botany?' I said, deliberately nudging the Bishop to no effect.

'The study of plants,' she said, tapping her fingers together again as if she had just described something utterly thrilling.

'Not really,' I said with a slight curl of my lip. 'Does that matter?'

'Not in the least,' she said. 'Not in the least.'

2

THE GLASSHOUSE

Oscar had not seen his father for nearly two years and they sat together as virtual strangers in the morning room, the slow, insistent beat of a hammer audible in the background. His father linked his long fingers together in his lap, tapping the thumbs in time with the hammer.

'How is school?' he said with a broad smile that Oscar found unaccountably annoying.

'School is well enough, Father,' he replied.

His father's smile quivered a little at the coldness of Oscar's response, but only momentarily. Algernon Bentley-Harrison had faced down tigers in the forests of Bhutan and fought off the enthusiastic attentions of headhunters in New Guinea; cheerfulness in the face of adversity was his stock-in-trade.

'Well enough?' said Mr Bentley-Harrison. 'Don't you have anything to report at all?'

'I'm not a scholar, sir,' said Oscar, 'if it is academic achievements you are hoping to hear about.'

'Nonsense. You're a very intelligent boy.'

'I didn't mean to say that I was not intelligent, Father. I just meant that I do not have whatever love of words, of books and numbers, it takes to be a scholar. My interests lie elsewhere.'

'As do my own, my boy,' said his father with a conspiratorial nod. 'I share your impatience with the confines of the classroom. There is so much more of interest in the world than can ever be contained in even the most comprehensive of libraries. That is what takes me to the ends of the earth, Oscar. It is the search for knowledge! It may seem a rarefied species of knowledge, certainly – but when you are of an age to accompany me, you too will see the importance of the botanical collections I have –'

'But Father,' interrupted Oscar with a sigh, 'I have no interest whatsoever in flowers.'

If Oscar had slapped his father round the face, it

could not have had a more profound effect. Flowers were Mr Bentley-Harrison's life, his passion.

Mrs Bentley-Harrison had once joked at a dinner party that she was not at all sure which her husband would rush to save first should there be a fire – his wife and son or his precious orchids. The guests had laughed, but there was a bitter aftertaste to the joke for the Bentley-Harrisons; they both knew there was no doubt about it: Algernon would save the orchids first.

'No *interest in flowers?*' said Mr Bentley-Harrison. 'But . . . but . . . I do not understand. You've always been interested in them in the past.'

'No, Father,' said Oscar, shaking his head but looking away with a sullen expression. 'I've tried to tell you often enough, but you wouldn't listen.' He turned to look at his father. 'You never listen, sir.'

Mr Bentley-Harrison's fingertips moved to his temples and began to describe concentric circles in his pale skin.

'But it has long been my dream that you and I –'

'That's just it,' said Oscar. 'It has been *your* dream, Father. It was never mine. You've never once asked me what I want to do with my life!'

This last sentence came out a little more loudly and a little more aggressively than Oscar had intended, so he was surprised when, instead of chastising him, his father merely stared silently into his lap and solemnly lowered his hands.

'Father?' said Oscar, when Mr Bentley-Harrison had still not responded after what seemed like several minutes.

'And what is it that you would rather do with your life?' said his father, without looking up. Oscar had never heard him talk in that way before. His voice sounded cold and mechanical. 'Eh? Come, let us hear what it is you intend as your life's work.'

'I should like to start my own business,' said Oscar. 'I should like to open a shop like the one Grandfather had when he started out.'

'A shop?' said Mr Bentley-Harrison slowly, as if he were trying a strange and foreign word for the very first time. 'A *shop*?'

Algernon Bentley-Harrison's father had owned a shop. Algernon had been forced against his will to work there until he had begged his mother to allow him to go away to university. His refusal to follow his father into the business had been a terrible disappointment to the old man. It looked as though the Fates were finally going to punish Algernon Bentley-Harrison for his disloyalty.

'Grandfather and I talked often about me starting

20

up the old business. He gave me lots of good advice. I shouldn't need a great deal of money, Father, and we have so very much.'

Mr Bentley-Harrison looked at his son. It was true that the old man had taken a special interest in the boy and infected him with his commercial zeal. It was also true that since the old man had died and Algernon had sold the business, they did indeed have an awful lot of money. But he was not about to see it used to such pedestrian ends.

'I'm afraid I need the money, Oscar,' said his father. 'The new glasshouses are very expensive, both to build and to maintain. They have to be constantly heated to very specific temperatures, you see.'

'But Father –'

'And I have earmarked most of the money to finance further expeditions in search of new species with which to stock the new buildings, expeditions I had hoped you might accompany me on, Oscar.'

'You're spending all of Grandfather's money on yourself?' said Oscar, his voice now as cold as his father's.

'It is my money now, Oscar,' he replied. 'But in answer to your question, I am spending my father's money on the quest for knowledge, on the advancement of science. There can be no finer use to which it could be put.'

Father and son looked at each other for some moments before Oscar scraped back his chair and got to his feet.

'Excuse me, Father,' he said as Mrs Bentley-Harrison entered the room. 'I have some school work to do.'

'Oscar?' said his mother, seeing his tight-lipped expression. 'Is everything all right?'

'Quite all right, Mother,' he replied.

'Algernon?' she said, turning to Mr Bentley-Harrison as her son walked out of the room.

'Everything is well, my dear,' he said with a bitter smile. 'Please don't fuss so. The boy is old enough to understand that he cannot have everything he wants.'

He picked up the copy of The Times on the table and began to read, while his wife remembered how, long ago, she too had learned that particular lesson.

Oscar had told her that he was going to inform his father of his desire to open a shop, and she could sympathise only too easily with Oscar's lack of enthusiasm for Algernon's obsession. She had no interest in botany either.

This would have shocked her husband even more than his son's admission, for she had feigned an interest for nearly twenty years now, hoping that if she shared his passion, their marriage might become something more than the loveless match it truly was. In the end, she had settled for being an invaluable assistant and attentive audience. Love was for books, she had concluded. Love was for other people.

Oscar, meanwhile, had gone to his room, striding with a fury that burnt like ice, and stood at the window, staring out. He could see the builders milling about as they put the finishing touches to his father's monstrous glasshouse in preparation for the precious plants that would soon arrive.

Oscar had a vivid image of his father showing his fellow botanists around his new realm, waving his hands this way and that, while his audience sighed approvingly and muttered jealously. Suddenly Oscar knew that the only thing in the world that mattered to him was to make that image a fantasy, to stifle his father's smug grin before it was even born.

A week later and the work was complete. The windows dazzled in the sunlight and a simulacrum of a jungle coiled and billowed in the Turkish-bath steam-heat inside the glasshouse.

Oscar saw less and less of his parents once the builders had left. Plants his father had been forced to grow elsewhere due to their size had been delivered and dragged and carried across the lawns and placed with care and attention he had never received.

Oscar's mother followed his father everywhere among the cast-iron columns, ceaselessly jotting in a huge notebook as she was given instructions on the needs of each plant. Oscar's needs had never been so assiduously noted or tended to.

These plants were like cuckoo chicks in the nest. Oscar hated them. He feared them. He imagined them growing and multiplying in the tropical heat of the glasshouse, growing and spreading, their coiling tendrils twitching and trembling.

To make matters worse, Oscar's father seemed to have a particular fondness for plants of the most revolting appearance. Only the previous day, he had shown Oscar a plant that he had discovered on his trip to the jungles of South America the year before.

'Have you ever seen anything like it?' he said.

'No, sir,' Oscar replied. He had not. The plant

was spectacularly ugly.

'I have never come across another plant that grows so fast and with such vigour. Why, I think that if we stood here long enough, we might almost see it growing with our own eyes.'

The plant was already huge. It had a fat central stem topped by a bulbous crown. The plant was dark green, but Oscar noticed that it also had thin blood-red veins running through it. There was something so utterly repulsive about its appearance that he had to quell a desire to back away.

The plant had sent out tendrils to coil and climb through the branches of neighbouring trees, and from each of these hung a curious dull-green sphere.

'Are they fruit or flowers?' said his father as he pointed them out. 'We just don't know. We shall have to wait and see, shan't we, eh? I can't even be certain what phylum of plant life this is. I know you say you have little interest in botany, my boy, but surely this must whet your appetite. It's fascinating, is it not?'

Oscar did not share his father's curiosity, but at least this plant was merely ugly. Others were poisonous, and the glasshouse positively bristled with needle-sharp thorns and saw-like serrations.

He couldn't wait to get out of there and away from his father, away from those revolting plants.

His feelings of resentment for his father's obsession, his disgust at the plants and the fetid, stultifying atmosphere of the glasshouse surged together into a kind of nausea.

If Oscar was to be denied what he wanted in life, then he would see how his father enjoyed having his dreams crushed.

Oscar was feeling rather pleased with himself. He had surprised himself with his own ingenuity. He felt a little taller now that he had taken charge of his own fate. He was sure that his grandfather would have been proud of him.

He had discovered that just a small amount of salt in the water used to spray the leaves of his father's precious plants would have the most disastrous effect.

And there was such a delicious pleasure in seeing his father actually spraying the poison on to his own plants.

Mr Bentley-Harrison was inconsolable when his prized orchids shrivelled and died mysteriously. The symptoms did not quite match anything in his books. He was baffled. He was wretched. Oscar had to stop himself gloating.

And if he ever felt the slightest ounce of remorse he simply had to remember his father's cold refusal to even discuss his desire to go into business.

Oscar was clever. He did not overdo the salting of the water and made sure that he added the salt only before the watering was done.

Watering cans and spray pumps were washed out and then new ones bought, but still the mysterious withering continued. Plant after plant succumbed. Oscar's father grew more and more despondent.

He refused any of the gardeners or servants access to the glasshouse and forbade Oscar or his mother to touch the plants in case they were inadvertently transmitting some as yet unrecorded disease. Oscar did not need to be asked twice. He had no desire to touch those disgusting plants.

It became harder to salt the water now that his father had taken personal control over every aspect of watering and feeding, but that just made the accomplishment of the task all the more rewarding.

Some days had passed since his last salting trip and Oscar was keen to get into the glasshouse to carry out his work. He had not seen his parents since breakfast. His father had taken even less interest in Oscar as he devoted himself utterly to trying to resuscitate his precious plants.

Oscar assumed they were in the glasshouse and waited impatiently for them to reappear so that he might slip in and wreak some more damage.

But no one could spend so much time in that sweathouse without a break. Oscar had sat near the door for hours now. They must be elsewhere. In any case, all he had to do was check.

Oscar wandered into the glasshouse, trying very hard to appear carefree. Almost as soon as he did so, he was struck by the fact that the air seemed even more oppressively humid than usual.

But it was more than that. There was a smell: a sweet, intoxicating smell he could not place. It was a rich and heady perfume, a perfume he did not recognise but which pulled him on, like a bee to a rose.

Turning a corner, he saw his parents and muttered a curse. They were standing beside the huge, ugly plant his father had shown him weeks before. His father had his back turned to him.

It was not until Oscar went closer that he noticed that his father's feet did not quite reach the ground. He appeared to be levitating, hovering about two or three inches from the floor. Then Oscar noticed a six-inch length of thorn sticking out of his father's back.

He stepped forward and saw that both his parents were skewered by huge thorns which seemed to have leapt from the earth and killed them both.

The thorn that had murdered his mother had driven itself through her notebook, pinning it to her chest. She too dangled a few inches from the air, held aloft by the thorn.

Both parents stared ahead, eyes open, mouths agape – a look of shock on his mother's face, a look more like wonder on his father's. Limply hanging in front of each of them was one of the plant's strange fruits or flowers, but now they looked like split and deflated balloons.

Oscar's heart thundered in his chest. He was shocked. Horrified. But he was surprised at how quickly these feelings began to disappear.

Oscar would never have actually wished his parents dead. Absolutely not. But neither, he was suddenly sure, would he miss them so very much. And any sadness he felt would be eased by the knowledge that Grandfather's money would now pass to him in its entirety and he would fulfil his dream of opening a shop.

There was something rather wonderfully ironic about his father falling victim to one of his own stupid plants. Despite all his mollycoddling, despite all the money he had lavished on them, still these plants did not return his love.

Oscar looked at his mother again and was shocked to see that inside her open mouth a tiny shoot was emerging. He shivered. The plant was growing inside her. Was she feeding it?

Oscar didn't want to think about it. He would call a servant and fetch the police or a doctor, or whomever one called in a situation like this. Then he saw his mother's eyes flicker and blink. Good God: she was still alive! Perhaps his father was too.

Oscar instinctively took a step forward but checked himself. No. No. He must not go near that plant. Too dangerous. She might be alive but she was beyond help, he told himself. They both were.

He would fetch a servant. In a little while. No purpose would be served by hurrying. Oscar tried unsuccessfully to stop himself thinking of the shop he would open with the money he would inherit, money that now would not be wasted on these hellish plants. He backed away and something touched the back of his head.

He spun round, expecting to see the horrified face of one of the servants, but saw instead one of the strange green fruits.

Before he had to time to register that this one was intact, it burst, releasing a fine dust of spores into his face – his nose, his mouth, his eyes.

Something in the spray of spores was paralysing him, but while he could still move his arms, he reached out to the tendril from which the fruit hung. It was covered with long white hairs. As soon as he touched one, there was a noise like a whip being cracked, and a powerful blow hit Oscar in the chest, just below his heart.

In spite of its force, the blow did not knock him over, because it had been dealt by a two-foot-long thorn that sprang up from the roots of the dreadful plant with startling speed and with the shocking snap of a mousetrap. The thorn impaled him and then held him in its grip.

Oscar wondered fleetingly whether he was dead, but he knew that he was not. Neither was he in pain. Something in the spores or the thorn had anaesthetised him.

But though he did not feel pain, he was, however, aware of the tendril that had already begun to emerge from the thorn, a tendril that in only a matter of hours would emerge from his mouth and, as he already saw, looking towards his mother out of the corner of his eye, would open up into a

small and rather lovely flower of a deep and irides-
cent blue.

When the story came to an end I gasped involun-
tarily. I felt as firmly held in its grip as Oscar had
been by that terrifying plant, as paralysed as he and
his poor parents had been.

I had a horribly clear picture in my mind of that
last fateful scene. I seemed to feel the oppressive
heat and stale atmosphere of that glasshouse. I
could see every leaf and tendril of that murderous
plant and smell the scent from its blue flowers.

I also had the distinct impression that there was
someone else present – someone in the dappled
shadows of the glasshouse. But as sharp as the
image had been, it disintegrated in seconds and was
gone, like a drawing inscribed in sand and washed
away by the incoming tide.

The effect was oddly debilitating. I felt exhausted.
It was as if listening to the tale had been a physical
rather than an imaginative act. My mind reeled and
my body seemed depleted of energy. It was as
though I was recovering from a run rather than
recalling the details of a story I had just been told.

The Woman in White smiled, clearly quite taken by the effect the story had wrought upon me and, feeling self-conscious, I avoided her eyes and looked out of the carriage window.

I must confess it was not quite the story I had been expecting. I had very limited experience of the fairer sex, but neither of my mothers – my natural one or the usurper I had left at the station – had ever had the slightest inclination towards stories of the macabre.

I was intrigued: intrigued and more than a little uncomfortable. I was troubled both by the grisly tale and the relish with which it had been told by a woman who, in every other respect, seemed to be most prim and proper and more at home at a church fete.

There was something fascinating about this woman. I hardly knew what to say, and I was sure that my expression bore the evidence of my confused emotions.

I feigned a sudden interest in brushing a crease from my trouser leg, before looking round at my fellow passengers. The Farmer, the Surgeon, the Bishop and the Major all slept on.

'How can people sleep so soundly in the middle of the day?' I said, a touch disapprovingly.

'Perhaps they are tired,' said the Woman in White.

'But we have only just begun our journey.'

'Perhaps,' she said again, turning to the sleepers with a sad smile. Then she turned back to me, leaned forward and tapped my knee.

'You look quite tired yourself, young man,' she said with concern.

'Me?' I said. 'Tired? No. Not at all.'

'Really?' she said.

I blinked against the heaviness in my eyelids and tried my best to appear alert, no doubt looking a little – and perhaps comically – wide-eyed. The Woman in White smiled again and leaned back into her seat.

'I have another story, if you have the energy to listen.'

'I assure you I am quite awake,' I replied.

'But I wouldn't wish to force it on you,' she said. 'Maybe you thought my story inappropriate – for a lady to tell and for one so young to hear. I don't wish to offend you.'

I was quite certain that she was not at all concerned what I thought and was in no way desirous of my good opinion. On the contrary: I was as equally sure that she was rather enjoying unsettling me.

'You have not offended me in the least,' I said.

Once again I looked at the other occupants of the carriage, willing one of them to awake and save me from another of this peculiar woman's tales. When I turned back to face her, the Woman in White was looking at me with such an expectant expression I felt obliged to say something.

'And what is this story about, miss?'

'I can tell you that it concerns two boys and a barrow. I think you will enjoy it.'

'Two boys and a barrow?' I said wearily, wishing that I could politely retract my agreement to listen to it. 'A wheelbarrow?'

'No,' she said. 'Not a wheelbarrow. But I mustn't spoil the tale by too much introduction . . .'

3

THE ISLAND

Henry Peterson opened the dormer window of the bedroom he shared with his brother Martin. They had arrived at the cottage late the previous evening, owls hooting unseen among the silhouetted oak trees, and this was his first real look at the view.

The cottage belonged to their father's mother, who had recently passed away. The boys had never been close to their grandmother and Henry had no recollection of ever having been to this house, though he was told he had been there when he was a little boy and Martin was still a baby.

Their father had fallen out with his mother

many years before and they had barely spoken since. To Henry, it was almost as if his grandmother had already died years ago, and so he felt no great sadness at her actual death, save for a vague sense of regret for something that had been kept from him and now would never be his.

Henry leaned out of the window. Bees were buzzing among the yellow roses on the climber that clung to the wall on either side and hung heavily from above. He looked out across the garden. There was a small orchard in front of him and a kitchen garden to his right with beans or peas coiling round tall canes. Birds were twittering in the tree tops. The house had its back set into a hill and the whole of Wiltshire seemed to stretch out before him: he could see for miles.

Beyond the shaggy hedge that bordered the grounds of the cottage was a huge field of green barley. A warm southerly breeze was sending waves through it, and the great swathe of barley surged and ebbed and rippled like a wide green ocean. Henry was hypnotised by it.

'What are you looking at?' said his brother Martin sleepily, as he sighed and stretched like a cat coming out of its nap.

'I'm just thinking that we should get out of this

house and go for a look around,' said Henry, without turning round. 'It's a glorious day. Father says there are badgers down the lane.'

'Look here, give a man a chance to wake up, won't you?' said Martin, sinking back into bed. 'Badgers or no badgers.'

Henry shook his head and grinned.

'You won't be able to lounge around all day like some sort of idle peasant when you come up to my school, you know,' he said. 'Old Hinkley will have your guts for garters.'

'That's all the more reason for enjoying it while I can. And I'm on holiday in any case, so I can stay in bed for as long as I like.'

'Oh no you can't!' said a voice from the corridor outside.

Their father opened the door, poked his head round and told them in no uncertain terms that they were to get up, get dressed and get out, because he and their mother needed to sort the house out. After all, that was the whole reason for being there. He told them that they were on no account to bother anyone and they weren't to trespass on the farmer's land.

So, much to Henry's delight, the boys were up and breakfasted and within half an hour of their father's appearance at the bedroom door, they were walking down the garden path, crickets chirruping in the long grass around them.

'So,' said Martin with a cavernous yawn, as they sauntered down the lane in the shade of a high hedgerow. 'What are we going to do?'

'I don't know,' said Henry breezily. 'Just explore, I suppose.'

'Doesn't seem a lot to explore,' said Martin sulkily, still begrudging his rude awakening. 'Just country-side everywhere.'

Henry laughed and pushed his brother sideways. He knew it wouldn't take much to get Martin going and, sure enough, Martin laughed and pushed him back.

The boys eventually came to a break in the hedge and Henry realised they were alongside the huge barley field he had seen from the window.

'Come on,' said Henry. 'Let's go to the island.'

'Island?' said Martin, looking round. 'What island? What are you talking about?'

'That island over there,' said Henry. 'I saw it from the house. I know it's not in water but it's an island all the same. Better, actually, because we won't get wet going there.'

'What about Father?' said Martin. 'He told us not

to go on the farmer's land.'

'The farmer isn't going to mind,' said Henry blithely. 'Besides, Father is going to be too busy sorting out Grandmother's junk to be bothered about what we do.'

'Even so . . .' said Martin with a glance back towards the cottage.

'Come on, Martin,' said Henry with a grin. 'Let's have some fun.'

Negotiations between the brothers often took this form: Henry the adventurous one, Martin the sensible one. But they almost always ended the same way too. Martin almost always relented.

'All right, then,' said Martin. 'But if some farmer appears with a shotgun, I'm telling him it was your idea.'

'Agreed,' said Henry with a grin, slapping his brother on the back. 'To the island!'

While Martin felt obliged to restrain his brother from following his foolhardy nature unchecked and to at least point out the inherent dangers of Henry's plans, nevertheless having voiced these concerns and been won over in spite of them, he would become as enthusiastic as Henry – perhaps even more so.

The boys set off into the field, wading through

the barley. The sun shone down and made the whole scene shimmer. The sky was deep blue and cloudless, the island a dark green silhouette. A sky-lark sang excitedly above them, seemingly the only sound in the waking world, and a primrose-yellow butterfly fluttered lazily past.

Henry was surprised at how long it took to reach the island and, as they finally approached it, he realised that it was much larger, and the trees much taller, than they had appeared from the bedroom window.

The two boys clambered out of the barley and up the steep sides of the island, using the roots and trunks and drooping branches of the trees for support. Henry was wondering to himself what kind of trees they were, when Martin called out, as if in answer, from nearer the summit of the island.

'These are yew trees,' he said. 'Like the one in the churchyard at home.'

Henry nodded. Martin was right. They had played in that churchyard yew since they were tiny and the wood was satin smooth, polished by the attentions of so many children over the years.

These yews seemed untouched and their bark was patchy like that of a plane tree, but rust-red and flaking off. The trunks and branches formed a kind

of cage, concealing the summit of the island fro
view. Martin was the first to claim it as his own.

'I'm the king of the castle,' he sang, 'and you're the dirty rascal!'

'Pipe down, Martin,' said Henry. 'You'll have the farmer on us. We're supposed to be spies, you know. Spies don't sing at the top of their voices.'

'I'm the king of the castle,' repeated Martin in a slightly louder and more enthusiastic voice, 'and you're the dirty – aaaargh!'

Punctuating Martin's plaintive cry was a grating, crumbling sound, and when Henry looked up he was shocked to see that Martin had disappeared. He leapt forward as a cloud of dust drifted towards him, stinging his eyes.

'Martin?' he called. 'Martin? Where are you?'

'I'm here,' came the pained response. 'Blasted thing's hollow and I've – ow, oww! – fallen in.'

Henry could see this for himself now that he had reached the summit of the island. It was not a hill he was standing on at all, but some kind of chamber.

'Are you all right?' said Henry.

'I think so,' Martin replied, shrugging himself loose from some fallen stones and rubbing his hair to clear it of dirt. 'Bruised my leg a bit, that's all.'

Henry, jumping down to
zing the big red weal appearing

rse.'

this place, do you think?' said Henry. 'An
e?'

that, here?' said Martin with a snort. 'In the
middle of a ruddy great field? Long way to come for
your ice.'

'Well, not an ice house then,' said Henry, a little
annoyed at Martin's tone. 'What then?'

'Don't ask me.' Martin winced as he inspected his
leg.

'Hey,' said Henry. 'What's that?'

Henry stooped down and moved a stone slab and
both boys recoiled together as they registered what
was revealed.

At their feet lay bones half concealed.

'It's part of an animal skeleton,' said Henry nonchalantly. 'It must have been here for ages. It looks
ancient.'

'I can see that,' said Martin. 'What kind of animal
is it?'

'I don't know,' said Henry. 'Badger maybe?'

Henry stooped down again and moved some
more of the stones, partially revealing the torso of

the skeleton. It was then that they saw the metal spike.

Jabbed between the creature's ribs and clearly going straight through the animal's body, was a spear about four feet long. It must have been made of copper, or something like it, because it was now green with verdigris. Henry went to grab it.

'No!' hissed Martin. 'We shouldn't. It's wrong.'

'Don't be such a baby,' said Henry. 'He's hardly going to complain, is he? Anyway, I only want to have a look.'

Martin clutched his brother's arm.

'Leave it alone, Henry,' he said. 'It doesn't belong to us.'

'It doesn't belong to anyone,' said Henry. 'Or at least, no one who's alive. Whoever speared this creature must have died a long time ago.'

'But why?' said Martin.

'Why what?' said Henry with an exasperated sigh.

'Why spear this animal and then build this place over the top?'

'Who knows?' said Henry. 'It was probably a religious thing. You know – pagans and all that.'

Martin suddenly clapped his hands.

'I know what this place must be,' he said, casting

a glance at the animal bones. 'It's a burial mound. You know – a barrow. Like in the book Father gave us. Remember?'

Henry nodded. Martin was right. There had been an illustration of a burial mound, showing different views: one from the outside, a diagram as if it had been sliced open and an imaginary illustration of what the dead man might have looked like inside with all his grave goods. This one appeared to be a similar construction.

'But barrows have warriors and kings in them,' said Henry. 'This one has a dead animal. Any idea what sort of animal it is yet?'

'I don't know,' said Martin. 'I still think we should leave things be.'

But Henry was on his haunches again, moving stones from around the skeleton to see if there was anything else of interest.

'We ought to fetch Father,' said Martin, trying to restrain him. 'Or the farmer.'

Henry shrugged him away.

'Aren't you just a bit curious?' he said.

'Of course I am,' Martin replied. 'But we don't know anything about archaeology. Let's go and get Father.'

'We will,' said Henry. 'We will. All I'm saying is,

let's see if we can't find out a little for ourselves and then tell them. This could be big news. Why should they take the credit? After all, it was you that found it.'

'I suppose so . . .' said Martin hesitantly.

Henry had already moved enough debris to see the skeleton of the animal more clearly. The head was missing. He crouched down to have a better look; Martin did the same.

'Some sort of dog maybe?' said Martin in a voice that made it more question than statement.

Henry frowned. If it was a dog, it must have been a strange-looking one – but then, thought Henry, it was a long time ago and they must have had different kinds of dogs then. It stood to reason. It was Martin who noticed the claws.

'Look at those,' he said with a whistle. 'What kind of dog has claws like that? It's more like a cat.'

Henry said nothing. Martin was right. It did look more like a cat, but even then the claws were more curved somehow. They reminded Henry of the talons of a hawk, though these were much bigger. He had never seen an eagle's claws, but he guessed these must be fairly similar.

'I think we should go now,' said Martin.

'Not yet,' said Henry. 'Let's at least uncover the

whole of this beast first.'

'And then we'll go?' said Martin.

'Then we'll go,' said Henry absent-mindedly.

The two boys scrabbled about in the rubble in the floor of the barrow, throwing up clouds of dust that made their eyes sting and forced them, coughing wildly, to leave its confines for a breath of air. Both laughed at the other's dusty white hair.

When the cloud their excavations had caused finally subsided and they had both coughed and spat their mouths free of dirt, they returned to see the results of their work.

There below them was the headless, but otherwise complete, skeletal outline of a beast that was, if anything, less recognisable for being more revealed. Pinned to the earth by its green copper spear, like a bug in a specimen case, was the body in all its strange entirety.

How could they ever have thought it was a dog? The torso was too long for that and the legs were completely wrong. And the tail was more like that of a lizard or a crocodile. It took a little while before either brother could think of anything to say.

'Perhaps it's not real at all,' said Martin, after they had studied it for a few moments. 'Perhaps they have put some parts of different animals together to make a weird creature.'

'But why would they do that?' said Henry. 'In any case – look at the skeleton. It all fits together.'

'It must be some kind of creature that doesn't exist any more,' said Martin decisively. 'You know – something everyone thought was just made up. Like a dragon or something.'

'Not a very big dragon, but even so,' said Henry, warming to this idea. 'Yes! And we've found it! Imagine that, Martin. We'll be famous!'

Henry reached out to grab the spear.

'What are you doing?' said Martin.

'I want to have a better look at this,' he said. 'I want to see the point.'

'I don't know, Henry,' said Martin.

Henry took a deep breath. He could feel one of Martin's irritating lectures coming on.

'What's the matter?' he said. 'It's not like it belongs to anyone. It can't possibly hurt to have a look.'

'It belonged to somebody once,' said Martin.

'That hardly matters now, does it?' said Henry with a laugh.

Martin scowled.

'It's still stealing, Henry,' he said. 'You know it is. Besides, I think there's something pretty odd about this place. Why is that animal here? Why build this thing over it with that spear stuck through it like that? Leave it alone.'

Henry sighed and forced a smile.

'I'm not going to steal it,' said Henry. 'I'm just going to have a look at it. As soon as I've had a look at the point we'll leave it here and go and fetch Father. Then he can do whatever one is supposed to do. Write a letter to the British Museum or who knows what. How about that?'

Martin considered this for a moment, but after weighing it all up, he shook his head.

'I'm going back to Grandmother's cottage,' he said. 'I really don't think you should be touching that thing. I don't like it here.'

And with that he began to scrabble out of the hole he had made in the roof.

'Martin!' shouted Henry. 'Martin! Don't be a boring girl. Come back!'

But Henry knew very well that once Martin's mind had been made up, no amount of shouting, cajoling or bullying would change it.

'I'm only going to have one tiny look!' he shouted after him.

But there was no reply and, without Martin beside him, it suddenly seemed a little darker in the barrow.

Henry grabbed the spear with both hands and tried to pull it out. It would not budge. He cursed Martin under his breath for leaving. It would have been so much easier if they had both pulled.

He sat back to catch his breath. And that was when he saw it, covered in dust in a dark corner of the barrow. He realised what it was straight away and left off trying to extract the spear to fetch it.

The head of the beast. It was big, far bigger than the size of the body would have suggested – but there could be no doubt it belonged, for it was as strange as the skeleton at his feet.

What had this creature been? What kind of thing had teeth like that: two rows of teeth? And the sharpness of them. Henry had never heard of any kind of animal with jaws like that. He whistled appreciatively.

Kneeling down, he placed the skull in position at the head of the skeleton to try to get some feel for what this strange creature must have looked like. As he got up to admire the completed skeleton, he grabbed the spear for support and it fell sideways.

His earlier efforts had evidently done their work. The spear was now free of the earth and the tip rested loosely among the ribs of the beast. Henry grinned and lifted it up for a better look.

The tip was less interesting than he had hoped. It seemed to have been made of iron and had corroded over the centuries so that it was black and scabrous and eaten away.

But however badly Henry wanted to show Martin that he was determined to investigate more, there was no way he was going to stay there on his own with that skeletal shark-toothed beast.

Henry clambered out of the barrow and called to Martin, whom he could see had deliberately dawdled, not wanting to leave his brother alone.

He called and waved the spear over his head, and Martin turned round and squinted into the sun, which was skirting the tops of the trees, throwing them and Henry into silhouette.

'What's that?' shouted Martin.

'It's the spear thing!'

'Put it back, Henry,' came the disappointing response from Martin. 'We should go home and tell Father, like you said.'

'You're such a bore sometimes, Martin,' Henry yelled back. 'I found the skull. You should see the teeth!'

'I don't care,' he said.

Henry sighed. Martin was as stubborn as a mule and there would be no changing his mind.

'All right,' said Henry. 'But I'm bringing this spear thing with me.'

'You said you were going to leave it there and fetch Father!'

'Well, I've changed my mind. I'm going to show him instead.'

'I don't see why you have to take charge of everything all the time, Henry!' shouted Martin. 'It was me who found it.'

'All you did was fall through the roof!'

'All the same,' said Martin, determined not to let his brother have everything his own way.

'Very well, then,' said Henry. 'You take it!'

With that, he threw the spear and it flew in a shallow arc, landing with a thud in the ground between them.

But Henry didn't see the spear land, because as he had released it into the air, there was a noise behind him that made him turn in alarm. Something large seemed to have shifted noisily nearby. He wondered if another part of the barrow had collapsed.

'Henry!' Martin shouted crossly. 'That was really stupid. You might have broken –'

Henry looked back across the barley towards his brother, but Martin was no longer there.

He stared around in confusion. It was as if Martin had simply vanished mid-sentence. But then he detected a movement some way off, near to where he had last seen his brother. The barley was being flattened in a narrow channel coming back in a wide arc towards the island.

Henry climbed down from the barrow with a grin.

'Very funny, Martin,' he said. 'But I can see you. Some Boy Scout you are!'

But the stalks of barley continued to fall and Martin made no reply. Henry shook his head indulgently and waited for his brother to get bored with this lark and reveal himself.

The trail of falling barley reached the island, but just round the back, beyond Henry's line of sight. A moment later he could see movement behind the yew trees and again he smiled at Martin's lack of stealth. But then he saw something move among the trees, something that made him shudder to his guts.

'Martin!' he screamed. 'Martin!'

The thing loomed out of the shadows into a clear patch on the barrow's ridge. It was big and on all fours. It was dragging something wet and ragged: it was dragging Martin – or something that had once been Martin – into the barrow.

Henry turned to run, sobbing to himself as he did so. He was not that far from the road. He was fast. He was the fastest in his year at school.

But then he thought of the spear. The spear must have been pinning that thing to the earth. Maybe if he could get to the spear . . .

Henry went back and tugged it from the ground. He pulled his arm back to launch the staff, but even as he did so, he could see the barley flattening in a path that hurtled towards him. The thing was on him before he could cry out.

A search was undertaken for the missing brothers. The farmer and two constables found their bodies and the circumstances of their discovery was so unusual it made The Times newspaper.

The boys were found in a partially collapsed barrow in the middle of a field. The farmer himself had no idea it was even there.

They seemed to have been attacked by a wild animal, and stories abounded for several weeks, with reports of sightings of everything from rabid dogs to escaped tigers. There was even an old tramp on the Avebury road who swore he saw a crocodile!

Near to the barrow detectives found a curious

iron-tipped copper-shafted spear, the significance of which is still being debated by experts at the British Museum.

'Oh my,' said the Woman in White when she had finished the story. 'Your face! I do believe I have shocked you.'

'Not shocked, no,' I said, trying to smile at her. But I was finding it difficult to rid myself of the rather vivid image of that gore-flecked creature dragging those unfortunate boys to its lair.

'I was merely a little taken aback by the subject matter of your story. I assure you, it would take more than that to shock me.'

She gave me a strange half-smile that I took to mean she did not altogether believe me.

'After all, it was only a story,' I said, determined to prove her wrong. 'All manner of terrible things may happen in a story. They may be startling at the time, but it passes. One gets caught up in the narrative, but the dangers aren't real, are they? Things happen in any way the storyteller chooses. It is all just made up.'

'Perhaps,' she said, turning to look out of the

window with a curious expression.

'You say "perhaps",' I ventured uneasily. 'Surely you're not suggesting that such a story might be true?'

She turned back to me and smiled, searching my face until I was forced to look away, unable to hold the intensity of her gaze. But she made no reply.

The light on the cutting had changed subtly and it created the illusion of the sides being even steeper than they had been before. Everything was as still as a picture: not a leaf moved, not a bird flew. Not even a bee or a butterfly disturbed the scene.

I pressed my face to the window again and tried to peer down the track, but could see nothing. The air of our compartment felt stale and I stood up and tried to open the window to create a little ventilation and to gain a better view, but the catch was jammed and after a few moments all I succeeded in doing was bruising my thumb. The Woman in White smiled benignly at me the whole time, as if she were watching a fish in a tank.

I sat down and looked at our fellow passengers to see if there were any signs of them waking up, but they remained as sound asleep as before. The Farmer's head was rather comically lolling on the Major's shoulder. The Bishop, who sat next to me, let out a plaintive moan. I took out my watch and gave it a shake, hoping to bring it back to life, but with no success.

'How long have we been here, miss?' I asked.

'Not long,' said the Woman in White cheerfully. 'As I have already told you.'

'But it feels like an age,' I said grumpily, a trifle annoyed at her refusal to actually tell me the time. *How long do they intend to just leave us here?* I thought to myself. *Are they simply going to keep us sitting about like fools?* I was sure Father would never have tolerated it, though I was less sure as to what ought to be done about it.

The Woman in White clasped her hands together in a rather maternal fashion and gave me a concerned, but patient, look.

'There is no sense in becoming agitated,' she said. 'It would be far better to simply relax, as these men have done. Are you not tired?'

The curious thing was that until she had said these words I hadn't in any way felt tired, but I had to confess that I did now feel most overpoweringly weary. My head felt heavy and my neck was suddenly aching with the effort of holding it up.

'Sleep if you wish,' said the Woman in White. 'I shall not be offended. Sleep.'

And sleep did seem deuced attractive in that instant. My eyelids had become great leaden weights that seemed to have no other course than to sink down over my eyes and usher in a dark and delicious slumber. Maybe the excitement of the journey and of starting a new school had affected me more than I realised. My eyelids fluttered, making the Woman in White flicker like a magic lantern show.

Then suddenly, instead of the Woman in White, I saw a vivid image of my stepmother, her face pale and wild as it had been when she awoke from her dream. I could almost hear her voice saying, 'Danger! Deadly danger!' It brought me straight back to a state of wakefulness.

'My dear boy,' said the Woman in White. 'Are you quite all right?'

'I am well, thank you,' I said. 'I was just thinking of my stepmother. She had a strange dream before I left her. She was troubled by it. She is very superstitious.'

'But you are not?' asked the Woman in White. 'Neither superstitious, nor troubled by her dream?'

'No,' I said. 'I think I have rather a distrust of superstition, actually. My stepmother likes to believe in omens and portents and the like, but I find it all a little foolish.'

'But did she not have some kind of premonition that something was to happen on your journey?'

'Why, yes she did – did I tell you that?' I said, wondering when that could have been.

'So you think it unimaginable that someone might be able to foretell the future?' she asked.

'I don't know,' I said with a grin. 'But I find it very hard to believe that, were that possible, such a gift might have attached itself to someone like my stepmother.'

The Woman in White did not return my grin.

'Perhaps it is not a gift in that sense,' she said. 'Perhaps it is more that a curtain that has hitherto been concealing other times or places – other worlds, if you like – is for a moment pulled aside. Perhaps it is a moment of revelation and nothing more.'

'A moment of revelation?' I asked, uncertain of what she meant.

'Yes,' she continued. 'A moment when, for whatever reason, a person is given access to a different kind of sight: a sight that allows them to glimpse another time or place. Do you not believe it to be possible?'

'Perhaps,' I said. 'I've heard of such people, of

course. But I suppose I always assumed them to be con men – or crazed. Do you believe it?'

She smiled.

'Oh, there is no question,' she said.

I was taken aback by the matter-of-factness of this reply.

'Have you had experience of it yourself, then?' I asked, instantly regretting giving her the opportunity to recount some garbled nonsense of the kind my stepmother was always coming out with.

'I have no need of such things,' she said with a little sigh and a smile.

'But . . .' I began, but got no further.

The image of that boy – Oscar – and his parents in the grip of that plant returned unbidden and with a frightening clarity and vigour. It made me jump as though electrocuted.

It was a curious thing, but I realised that listening to these stories was different to listening to any stories I had heard before. I felt myself actually there, as if I were a witness to the events being described. It felt as though, instead of listening to the words the Woman in White was saying, I was actually seeing images, hearing voices; it was like a dream, but at the same time more real than any dream.

'Are you sure you're all right?' said the Woman in White. 'You're looking rather pale.'

'I am quite well, miss, thank you,' I said.

But I was not feeling as well as I pretended. The carriage was awfully warm and stuffy. I got to my feet and tried to open the window again, but it still would not budge, despite repeated attempts.

I smiled at the Woman in White, cursing silently at my inability to perform this simple task. I was certain that I detected a trace of enjoyment at my discomfort in her cool smile.

Then, quite suddenly, I felt dizzy and had to reach out for the luggage rack to keep my balance while the carriage and all its occupants seemed to spin around me in a vortex.

'Can I be of assistance?' she said, rising to her feet and reaching out to me.

'No!' I said, more sternly than I had intended. But I really did not want to be mollycoddled by this strange woman.

Besides, there had been something about the way she had reached out to me that set my nerves on edge. No doubt, I thought, it was an effect of my light-headedness, but she seemed to move with a horrible fluency and speed that made me recoil.

I sank down into my seat and gradually the

spinning slowed and then stopped, though everything remained a little blurred. I focused on the Woman in White, who now looked the very picture of English reserve, sitting prim and demure, gazing out of the carriage window.

'We have been forgotten, surely,' I said, trying to regain my composure, and following her gaze out towards the cutting. 'How long have we been sitting here and not a single person has walked past, inside or out? It's a disgrace.'

I had no idea whether it was actually a disgrace, but I rather liked the sound of the words. My father would have said the same, I was sure of it. Why would she not just tell me the time? I gave the sleeping passengers a despairing look. These men might have had nothing better to do than sleep the day away, I thought, but I needed to get to London. Whatever the problem was, surely we should at least have been kept informed of any progress in resolving it.

I thought these things with some degree of passion, and it immediately brought on a recurrence of my dizziness. An intense pain stabbed my temples and I closed my eyes for a moment. When I reopened them, the Woman in White's face was alarmingly close to my own.

'I am certain everything will be quite all right,' she said, with a smile that seemed to say she was as happy to be there as anywhere and had all the time in the world.

'But I have things to do,' I said falteringly. 'I cannot simply sit here all day.' I threw a glance at my sleeping companions and deliberately raised my voice, hoping to rouse them. Was I the only person on this train with somewhere to be?

'Patience is a virtue,' she said.

'I had a governess who used to say that,' I said. '*Patience is a virtue. Patience is a virtue.* She was like a parrot – except not as pretty. Lord, how I hated her.'

I suddenly realised this might be construed as an implicit criticism of the Woman in White and blushed. She seemed to enjoy my unease.

'Were you frightful to your governess?' she asked.

'Well, I . . . I don't, er . . .' I burbled.

The truth was that I had indeed been frightful to my governess. I had made the poor woman's life a misery for no other reason than that I could.

She was treated as just another servant by my parents and in some ways, worse, for they had a grudging respect for the other servants – or, most of them at least. But the governess's work did not result in crisply ironed shirts or delicious desserts.

She was invisible when effective and an irritant when she failed in the most important of her tasks: to prevent my parents being in any way inconvenienced by me.

'The life of a governess is often an unhappy one,' said the Woman in White sadly.

'Do you speak from experience?' I asked, for though she had denied being a teacher there was something of the buttoned-up air of a governess about her.

'Bless you, no,' she said. 'I have never been a governess, though I have come to know a few over the years. Shall I tell you about one of them?'

'I don't –'

'Very well, then,' she said.

4

A NEW GOVERNESS

Amelia Spenser sat studying the elegant drawing room as a carriage clock on the mantelpiece struck the quarter hour. The room was tastefully and expensively furnished, and although drawing rooms were often feminine, there seemed a particular confidence in the femininity here, and in the house as a whole, of which Amelia thoroughly approved.

Mrs Rowland, her new employer, was dressed in the dour and sombre clothes she had taken to wearing since her husband had been posted to the wilds of Afghanistan in defence of the British

Empire. Their love was so strong that the parting felt like a kind of mourning, despite the long and tender letters she received.

Of late it had felt all the more so. She had heard nothing from her husband since his letter from Kabul telling her his cavalry regiment was to move on Kandahar. But that had been nearly two months previously. Yet still there was real warmth in her smile as she sat down opposite her new governess. These days she found any distraction from thoughts of her dear husband's plight a welcome boon.

'Your character was excellent, Miss Spenser,' said Mrs Rowland, by which she meant that Amelia's references were excellent; Mrs Rowland was yet to make a firm judgement on the girl's actual character and, in any case, was the kind of person who tried to think the best of everyone she met, something her husband found charming and infuriating in equal measure. 'I should think that the Fanthorpes were very sorry to see you go, my dear.'

'In truth, ma'am,' said Amelia, 'they had little need of me any more; all the children are away at school now. Major Fanthorpe is to rejoin his regiment in India and Mrs Fanthorpe is to accompany him. I hardly know how Mrs Fanthorpe will cope with such a climate; she is so . . . delicate.'

Mrs Rowland nodded, rather surprised that Amelia should venture an opinion on her previous employer, but content to let it pass this once.

'You are so very young, Miss Spenser,' she said. 'Great Nitherden was your first position as governess, was it not?'

'Yes, ma'am,' said Amelia. 'Major and Mrs Fanthorpe were friends of my father and were kind enough to give me my first employment. I owe them a great deal.'

And so she did. Had Amelia's father not saved Major Fanthorpe from the murderous attentions of a particularly well-armed sepoy in the storming of Delhi in '57, Miss Spenser would have had a very different character reference, one that spoke of her wild mood swings, her coldness towards the children and of her inappropriate and unrequited attachment to the Major himself.

'I am satisfied that you will be a marvellous friend to the children,' said Mrs Rowland. 'I hope you will be very happy with us.'

'I'm sure I shall, ma'am,' said Amelia.

'Now, Mary has shown you your room,' said Mrs Rowland. 'I trust that everything is satisfactory?'

'It is a lovely room, ma'am,' said Amelia. 'I shall be very comfortable.'

'Do you have any questions about your employment here?' said Mrs Rowland. 'Is there anything you would like to ask?'

'No, ma'am,' said Amelia. 'Your letter was very detailed.'

'Excellent,' said Mrs Rowland, standing up and holding out her hand. 'Then there is nothing left but for me to welcome you to Panton Manor.'

Amelia took Mrs Rowland's hand.

'Thank you, ma'am. When might I meet the children?'

'They are very excited about meeting you, Miss Spenser,' said Mrs Rowland. 'I thought we might all have lunch together and get to know each other then.'

'As you wish, ma'am,' said Amelia, hoping she had not made it too plain that she thought this a poor idea. She would have liked to meet the children in a more formal setting to ensure that they knew her expectations of them from the outset.

'I shall see you at twelve o'clock then, Miss Spenser. Perhaps you might like to take a walk in the gardens before lunch. They are looking rather lovely at the moment.'

'Yes, ma'am,' said Amelia. 'I should like that very much.'

The gardens were just as lovely as Mrs Rowland had promised they would be. A large lawn led down to a ha-ha with acres of parkland beyond.

Sheep lay with their lambs in the shade of countless trees, and a folly in the form of a tumbledown abbey crowned a hill to the west, its arched windows and castellated walls standing out starkly against an azure sky.

Feeling the need for shade, Amelia made for the shelter of the walled garden, where she found a bench in the shadow of a high brick wall on which a pear tree had been trained, its snow-white blossom buzzing and grumbling with bees.

A sunburnt gardener working nearby tipped his hat to her before getting on with his work, and Amelia pulled out her pocket watch and saw that she had ten more minutes to enjoy the peace and quiet before she had to meet her new charges, ten minutes in which to gather her thoughts so that she was in just the right frame of mind to give the correct impression. This was a fresh start and she was determined that it should all go exactly to plan from the beginning.

She closed her eyes. She could hear the rustling of the gardener as he filled his wheelbarrow with the offcuts from the shrubs he had been pruning, and then the diminishing rumble of the wheel on the shingle path as he took the load to the compost heap.

At the sound of footsteps returning, Amelia opened her eyes once more, expecting to see the gardener, but instead, standing at the end of the path beside the doorway through which the gardener must have disappeared, were three children: a boy of about ten years, another boy of about eight and a girl who was a little younger still. The younger of the boys stepped forward.

'Hello, miss,' he said. 'Are you our new governess?'

Amelia sat upright and straightened her skirt, embarrassed at having been caught in so relaxed a position.

'Hello, children,' she said. 'Yes, that is correct. I am Miss Spenser.'

'Are you?' said the girl, giggling and elbowing the boy at her side. 'That's nice.'

'Yes I am,' Amelia replied, her smile slowly disappearing.

They certainly wanted for manners, she thought.

'And who might you be?' asked Amelia.

'My name is Andrew,' said the younger boy. 'And this ugly creature is my sister, Cecelia – though everyone calls her Sissy.'

The older boy said nothing. When Amelia looked at him, he stared back with an arrogance she found both shocking and unnerving.

'And you must be Nathaniel,' she said, remembering that Mrs Rowland had given the names of her children in her letter. He grinned in reply.

The other children stared wide-eyed at her, then at each other and then back at Amelia.

'Not Nathaniel,' said Cecelia frowning. 'Daniel.'

Amelia winced with embarrassment at having made such a silly mistake. She always took particular care not to make errors in front of children. One must never let them know that one might be fallible. It wasn't good for discipline. How vexing! She was sure Mrs Rowland had said Nathaniel.

'You're home from school for the holidays?' Amelia asked Daniel.

But instead of giving a reply, the children merely turned and ran off along the path. Amelia frowned.

'Goodness,' she said to herself. 'I can see I'm going to have my work cut out for me here.' She glanced at her pocket watch. 'Oh my – look at the time. I mustn't be late for lunch. That would never do.'

When she looked up from her watch, she saw the gardener standing where the children had been.

'Sorry, miss,' he said. 'Did you say something?'

'Yes – no – I was talking to the children,' she said.

The gardener smiled and nodded.

'Those little 'uns giving you the run around already, then? I heard Daniel's name mentioned. You probably got more than you bargained for there, eh? Perhaps they ought to pay you extra.' The gardener winked.

Amelia did not much care for his over-familiar tone.

'The children have not in any way given me the run around, as you put it,' she said with a sniff. 'And should they attempt such a thing, they will find me equal to any challenge they might put before me.'

The gardener gave Amelia a long look that made her uncomfortable.

'I meant no offence, miss,' he said finally.

'As for Daniel,' said Amelia, getting to her feet. 'He will find me firm but fair.'

The gardener frowned and was about to speak when Amelia interrupted him.

'I'm sorry,' said Amelia. 'But I must be going to the house. I am expected for lunch. Good day.'

'Ma'am,' he said, with a tip of his hat, and went back to his work as if she were not there.

Amelia walked away with as much dignity as she could muster, determined to show this yokel that she had some breeding, even if he did not, but her efforts were undermined by having taken the wrong path and having to retrace her steps.

Amelia was sure she saw the gardener smirking as she passed him and she could feel the colour rising to her face as she walked towards the house.

'My dear Miss Spenser,' said Mrs Rowland. 'I fear you may have caught the sun.'

'I'm a little warm, ma'am, that is all,' said Amelia.

'It is very hot today,' said Mrs Rowland. 'Do come and sit down. Jane – pour Miss Spenser a glass of lemonade. Come, we will put you next to the children so that you can get a good view of each other.'

At the end of the dining table were the three children she had met in the garden. At her approach, Andrew and Cecelia got to their feet. Daniel remained sullenly and obstinately seated.

'How do you do, Miss Spenser,' said Andrew, as if they had not already met.

'How do you do,' said Amelia.

'You're a lot prettier than our last governess,' said Cecelia.

'Sissy, honestly,' said her mother. 'What a thing to say.' Mrs Rowland turned to Amelia with a conspiratorial smile. 'Though I'm afraid it's true. Miss Cartwright was rather plain.'

Amelia smiled but her attention was distracted. Something was moving about under the table and rubbing up against her legs. She gave a small kick and a large, long-haired ginger cat ran out.

'You know I don't like Molly in here while we're eating, Andrew,' said Mrs Rowland. 'The children dote on her, Miss Spenser,' she said, turning to Amelia.

Amelia smiled. Whether they doted on her or not, Amelia would see to it that the filthy creature was kept in the yard where it belonged. There was so much to do here. So very much.

During this whole encounter Daniel had neither moved nor spoken, but simply sat regarding Amelia with a look of such malevolent and haughty disdain that it took all her willpower not to discipline him that instant. Andrew noticed where she was looking and smiled.

'Oh, that's Daniel. He's not very good with strangers.'

Amelia smiled.

'I'm sure that Daniel and I will get along very well once he gets to know me a little better.'

Mrs Rowland smiled and reached out to touch Amelia's arm. Amelia thought that she detected a tear in her employer's eye.

'Oh my dear,' she said. 'I think the children are going to grow awfully fond of you, won't you, my lambs?'

'Yes, Mother,' said Andrew with polite enthusiasm.

'Now, I am going to leave you to get acquainted. I have a luncheon appointment with Mr Travers. He has some dull business that he wants to discuss and, tedious though it is, it must be done. Be good, my lovelies.'

Amelia began to rise to her feet as her employer stood up, but Mrs Rowland put her hand on Amelia's shoulder.

'Please,' she said with a smile. 'No need to stand, my dear. We are very informal here. I shall see you later this afternoon.'

Luncheon got underway. Amelia took it upon herself to direct the servants as they brought the food to the table, all the while watching Daniel with a growing sense of unease and anger. But though Amelia was disgusted by both Daniel's behaviour and the indulgence shown to him by her employer, she thought it wise to bide her time on this occasion. She wanted to see the true extent of the boy's delinquency.

As each course arrived, a portion rather smaller than those for the other children was placed in front of Daniel, but he did not touch a thing.

'Daniel doesn't seem to enjoy his food,' said Amelia to Andrew in a voice that she hoped might convey the entirely false impression that she had not the least interest in such things.

'Daniel's a very fussy eater,' said Andrew.

'Yes,' said Cecelia, with what Amelia thought was an unpleasant giggle. 'Very fussy.'

Daniel poked his tongue out at Cecelia.

Amelia was determined not to rise to the bait she felt was being laid in front of her. There would be time enough to deal with Daniel. It was clear by the degree of licence he was allowed by Mrs Rowland that this was neither the time nor the place.

But Amelia knew that if she was going to do the job for which she had been employed, then she was going to have to take control of the boy whose insolent stare she was artfully ignoring, before his influence poisoned the hearts of his siblings. Their behaviour was already showing the first signs of unruliness.

Each course was taken away from Daniel's place uneaten and Amelia silently wondered how Mrs Rowland allowed this nonsense. If she had no interest in the child's behaviour then surely she must have some concern for his health. No wonder the boy was so thin and and disagreeable.

Mrs Rowland said there was no expectation that Amelia should start work that day and that she should get settled into her new room, which was small but prettily decorated. It was next to the children's rooms and looked out on to the walled garden she had visited.

From the window Amelia could see Andrew and Cecelia playing on the lawn nearby. Daniel stood at the edge, in the shade of a holly tree. As she watched him, he slowly turned round to face her with an expression of utter contempt.

What an unpleasant little boy you are, she thought to herself. *But I can be unpleasant too, as you shall find out.* Nevertheless, the boy unsettled her more than she would have believed possible.

Amelia and Mrs Rowland dined together without the children, though her employer explained that in future they would all eat together. Amelia was pleased that she did not have to suffer a repeat of Daniel's appalling behaviour at luncheon. She was tired and was not at all sure that she could have borne it with the same quiet stoicism she had displayed then.

Mrs Rowland was gently probing in her questions about Amelia's time with the Fanthorpes, but Amelia had no difficulty responding with vague replies rather than outright lies. Her new employer was clearly a very nice person and Amelia was suddenly overwhelmed by a desire to help her. She felt an enormous rush of sympathy for this woman, left here on her own. She was clearly unable to cope with the behaviour that the children were exhibiting, most probably in response to their fatherless state.

She would save this household from disaster. She would help this woman take charge of her children once more and save those children – especially Daniel – from themselves. The young needed firm guidance. Amelia would provide it.

When she eventually said goodnight to Mrs Rowland and retired to her room, she felt it her duty to check on the children first. As she turned the door handle to Daniel and Andrew's room, she was filled with an intoxicating sense that that particular moment was the true beginning of her life among them.

The room was dark, but it didn't take long for her eyes to adjust to the gloom. There were two children in the room, but all was not as it should have been.

'What are you doing in here, Cecelia?' said Amelia. 'It is very late. And where, might I ask, is Daniel?'

Stifled giggles greeted this question and Amelia could feel her heartbeat quicken as she struggled to control her temper.

'I demand that you answer me this instant,' she hissed.

'He's not here, miss,' said Cecelia.

'He's never here at night, miss,' said Andrew.

'Never here at night?' said Amelia. 'What nonsense are you talking, you silly boy?'

'But it's true, miss,' said Andrew, very serious now. 'He likes to wander, doesn't he, Sissy?'

'Yes,' said his sister. 'Daniel loves to wander the house at night. He says he likes to know what everyone is up to.'

'Oh, does he now?' said Amelia. 'And what of your mother? What does she think of Daniel "wandering" as you call it?'

'Oh, she doesn't know,' said Andrew.

'I find that very hard to believe,' said Amelia.

'It's true, Miss Spenser,' said Sissy. 'We wouldn't lie to you. Would we, Andrew?'

'Oh no, miss,' said Andrew with great solemnity.

Miss Spenser was convinced they were mocking her. She snorted and pursed her lips, exasperated that the children would dare to sport with her in such a blatant manner. There was so much to do, she thought, so much to change.

'Where is he?' said Amelia hoarsely, moving towards Sissy. 'Where is Daniel?'

'We don't know,' said Andrew. 'Honestly we don't. Please don't talk to Sissy in that horrid voice. Daniel never tells us where he's going. He just goes and then he comes back. That's how he is. It's beastly of you to blame Sissy.'

'Beastly? Beastly?' Amelia paused to take a deep breath. 'I can see that I shall have my work cut out here, but let me tell you – and Daniel, if he is hiding behind the ottoman, as I suspect he is – that Amelia Spenser is not the sort of person to back away from a challenge: quite the reverse. I shall bid you goodnight.'

For all her strident tone, Amelia was surprised to

find that her hands were moist with sweat when she closed the door behind her.

There was something about these children that she found distressing. She had dealt with naughtiness and wilfulness before – what governess had not? – but these children were different somehow.

Andrew and Cecelia were far too headstrong and forward, but she felt confident that she could cure them of that if she could only tame Daniel. He was the key; she was sure of it.

But it was going to be difficult with Mrs Rowland evidently being the kind of parent who let her children run wild and then expected governesses and schoolmasters to tidy up after them.

As she brushed her hair, she heard a noise in the corridor outside her room. She walked to the door and pulled it open, glancing quickly to right and left.

But the glow of her candle did not create a great deal of illumination. A battalion of the Scots Guards could have been standing twenty yards away and she would not have detected so much as a brass button in that gloom.

Still, Amelia was sure that Daniel was there, watching, and she smiled a wry smile at his childish efforts to unnerve her, but the smile was more forced than she would have liked. She would deal with Daniel in the morning.

She stepped back and closed the door again and then gasped, almost dropping her candle, as she saw Daniel standing in the centre of her room.

'Get out this instant!' said Amelia, her free hand fumbling at the door handle until the door finally creaked open.

Daniel merely smiled and walked towards her. He paused and looked up into her face with cruel disregard, as though she were a fly he was about to swat. Then he nonchalantly walked past her and out of the room.

Amelia stood for a moment, her heart racing, and then she hurriedly shut the door, turning the key in the lock. She walked shakily over to her bed and sat down, taking long breaths to calm herself.

'I shall deal with you tomorrow, little boy,' she said to herself. 'Have no fear.'

Amelia slept rather fitfully that night, and she had to compose herself for nearly ten minutes before she felt able to join the family for breakfast.

She had persuaded herself that the best course of action was to have a meeting with Mrs Rowland, tell her of her concerns regarding the children and calmly, but firmly, explain that she must, as the children's governess, be allowed to take the lead in setting boundaries of behaviour.

But this resolution dissolved as Daniel once again ate nothing and stared at her throughout the meal with his usual look of contempt. Molly the cat rubbed herself up against Amelia's leg and she kicked out, making the cat squeal and leap from under the table, ears back, tail fluffed up.

'No, no!' said Amelia, throwing down her napkin with rather more force than intended and sending a teaspoon clattering across the table. 'This is insufferable!'

'My dear!' said Mrs Rowland. 'Is there something the matter?'

'I wonder at how you can ask such a thing,' said Amelia, her voice fluttering with frustration.

'But I don't understand,' said Mrs Rowland, looking concernedly at the children. 'If Molly upsets you this much –'

'This is not about Molly!' shouted Amelia.

Mrs Rowland frowned and waved away the parlour maid, who was standing staring open-mouthed at Amelia's outburst.

'Whatever is the matter, dear? Would you like to discuss it in private?' asked Mrs Rowland quietly.

'He is the matter, ma'am,' said Amelia, pointing to Daniel.

'Who?' said Mrs Rowland, looking baffled.

'Daniel, of course!' said Amelia in exasperation.

'Daniel?' repeated Mrs Rowland.

Cecelia giggled and Andrew kicked her.

'Ow!'

'Children go to your rooms,' said their mother.

'But Mother –' said Andrew.

'This instant,' said Mrs Rowland. 'I need to speak to Miss Spenser alone.'

'I should prefer it if Daniel stayed,' said Amelia in the severest tone she could muster. 'He roams about the house at night and even had the audacity to enter my room and behave in the most insolent manner.'

The children stopped in their tracks and stared back at the adults expectantly. Mrs Rowland put her hand to her mouth, looking at Amelia as if she were afraid of her suddenly.

'Sissy, Andrew – go to your rooms!' she said. 'Please do not make me ask you again.'

The children were not used to hearing such a harsh tone in their mother's voice and left the room without further complaint. Amelia looked at Daniel across the table, and he stared defiantly back. Mrs

86

Rowland rested on her hands as if in prayer and so it fell to Amelia to say something.

'I am sorry, ma'am,' she said. 'I should not have expressed myself so forcefully. But I feel that Daniel needs a firm hand or –'

'Miss Spenser,' interrupted Mrs Rowland. 'I think this nonsense has gone far enough.'

'I beg your pardon, ma'am?' said Amelia.

'At first I was delighted that you were sporting enough to indulge the children in their play, as I have done – possibly a little too readily since their father went away – but now I think you're upsetting them.'

'Upsetting *them*?' said Amelia, casting a vicious glance at Daniel, who smiled back. 'Is Daniel to be given free licence to treat me in any way he sees fit, then?'

Again Mrs Rowland raised her hand to her mouth, and Amelia was shocked to see tears filling her eyes.

'But my dear girl,' said Mrs Rowland. 'Daniel is the poor gypsy boy we took into our home two years ago. What his real name is, we never did know, for he was a mute and could not write.'

'Gypsy boy?' said Amelia, confused. She had noticed that Daniel was rather sallow-skinned, despite his paleness, and shared little resemblance to the other two children, but had thought little of it. 'But I don't follow you, ma'am.'

'The poor boy had been caught in a poacher's trap and his people had left him behind. He must have been in terrible pain and yet he made barely a sound. We took him in and did all we could for him. Oh, but he was such a wild little thing.'

'Was?' said Amelia. 'I'm afraid he still is. I commend you for your Christian charity in adopting this boy, ma'am, but the absence of any kind of manners or reasonable standards of behaviour seems to betray a lack of gratitude that –'

'But Daniel died, my dear,' said Mrs Rowland quietly. 'A year ago.'

Amelia stared at her employer, trying to make sense of what she was saying.

'What can you mean, ma'am?' said Amelia, pointing across the table. 'Then who is that?'

'Stop it! Stop it at once!' cried Mrs Rowland, getting to her feet. '*There is no one there!*'

Amelia looked across the table. Daniel grinned.

'But what do you mean? I can see him . . . I can see him sitting there!' shouted Amelia.

Mrs Rowland backed away, refusing to look in the direction of Amelia's shaking, pointing finger.

Tears were rolling down her cheeks.

'The children began to say that Daniel was with them sometimes when they played, and I, perhaps foolishly, indulged them. I could not see what harm it could do. I thought that it was their way of dealing with the loss. Many children have imaginary friends.'

'An imaginary friend?' said Amelia, staring at Mrs Rowland as the edge of her vision became greasy and blurred and began to slip away from her. 'But you told me about Daniel in your letter.'

'I told you about *Nathaniel*,' she said. 'Nathaniel. My eldest boy who is away at school.'

'Nathaniel?' said Amelia quietly. It was true. She remembered now. It *had* been Nathaniel in the letter. She felt dizzy. Her thoughts seemed to be spinning about like leaves in a whirlwind.

'Oh my dear,' said Mrs Rowland. 'I think I ought to contact your parents.'

'No . . . please . . .'

'I think I must insist,' said Mrs Rowland sternly. 'It is for the best. You are not yourself.'

Amelia looked back towards Daniel and saw, no matter how hard she stared, that his chair was empty. When she turned to Mrs Rowland again, her employer was already leaving the room.

Amelia had a curious shrinking sensation, as if, like Alice on her way to Wonderland, she was entering some new world where nothing would make sense. She searched her memory, hunting blindly back through the hours she had spent in the house looking for something that would make Daniel as real as he had seemed, but all she found were smirking gardeners and giggling children.

She felt Molly the cat playing with her shoelaces, but her legs were too weak to kick out this time. As if in a trance, she eased her chair back and lifted the tablecloth to shoo the creature away, falling backwards as she saw Daniel crawling out from the shadows under the table, a horrible grin on his face.

Mrs Rowland told friends later that the scream sounded like nothing she had ever heard before or would ever want to hear again, and that she had returned to the dining room to find the poor deluded girl wildly kicking out at empty air, as if the devil himself was coming for her.

She had sat down beside Amelia and held her in her arms, calling for a maid to fetch the doctor, who arrived within minutes and lost no time in sending word to the sanatorium at Bennington Priory. It was only two miles away.

Amelia's movements did gradually become less violent as they waited, but Mrs Rowland saw that the poor girl's face was a mask of terror still. She looked with such intensity that Mrs Rowland was compelled to follow her gaze, but she could see nothing but her own dear children, who had wandered into the room. Cecelia was holding Andrew's hand. Her other hand was by her side, her fingers curled, as if grasped by someone standing unseen beside her. Then, as silently as they had appeared, the children turned and walked away.

My storyteller sat back contentedly after her tale, with a tight, pursed little smile and sparkling eyes, as if she had delivered the most morally uplifting and instructive of sermons.

But I fear my expression must have been somewhat different. The image of that spectral boy was for some reason especially disturbing to me. I felt the need to discuss the story in order to exorcise it.

'So was the governess mentally disturbed, then?' I said after a pause.

'Well if she was, she is cured now,' said the

Woman in White with an alarmingly inappropriate chuckle. I frowned.

'I meant – was she perhaps hallucinating?' I persisted.

'You seek reassurance,' said the Woman in White with an expression a nanny might have used had I been four years old and scraped my knee. 'You seek comfort. You want there to be a rational explanation.'

All that she said was true, of course, and yet there was something in her tone of voice that made me prickle. But again, I found it hard to collect my thoughts as the feeling of fatigue returned unabated.

'Forgive me. You still seem to talk as though these were real events and not the happenings of a story,' I said. 'I was merely trying to make sense of the character and what she might have been thinking.'

'I see,' she said, but added nothing more.

A fly droned lazily past my face and collided drunkenly with the carriage window. It made several attempts to butt its way through this barrier and, having failed, flew off once more in confused circuits of the compartment. There was something mesmerising about following its meandering flight path.

It landed on the head of the Surgeon and began to wander across the sleeping man's forehead. I watched with a grin, fully expecting him to suddenly awake with comic flapping and spluttering at the irritation of the crawling fly.

But to my increasing astonishment, the fly continued its journey across the Surgeon's face with only the slightest twitch from the gentleman's eyebrow.

This slight twitch was enough, though, to persuade the fly to take flight, and it set off again on its ragged circuit of the compartment. Without looking, the Woman in White reached out and plucked the insect from the air.

She did this with such stealth that had the fly not disappeared, I might not even have registered the action. Again, without looking, she opened her hand and the fly dropped dead to the floor.

'I detest flies,' she said. 'You would think that I'd have become used to them by now, but I never have.'

It was such an extraordinary thing for anyone to do – let alone the prim young woman sitting before me – that I almost immediately began to doubt what I had seen, particularly as my eyelids were becoming heavy once more and everything seemed to be losing clarity. Had I imagined it, just as I had earlier imagined my stepmother? And yet the fly was on the floor, dead. There was no doubting that.

But remembering my stepmother made me once again feel that it was somehow vital that I stayed awake and alert. I had to keep talking. I had to keep my mind active.

'You don't appear to have much sympathy for the people in these tales,' I said, taking my eyes from the fly. 'If you will forgive my frankness, it seems a little *unfeminine*.'

'Does it?' she said with raised eyebrows. 'Dear me, but you have a lot to learn.'

'I simply meant that the feminine sex is more naturally caring.'

'And yet you find that irritating,' she said, 'when your stepmother is doing the caring.'

I frowned.

'I rather think I have said too much about my stepmother,' I said. 'Surely you must agree though: ladies are more predisposed to nurturing.'

'Perhaps. But girls can be quite vicious, you know,' she said.

I had to concede that this was true. A good friend of mine at school invited me to stay at his house one Easter holiday and his sister was vile. I have been wary of girls ever since.

'Girls can be particularly cruel to other girls,' she said. 'You are a boy and can never fully appreciate this. These matters are only exaggerated when girls are thrown together unwillingly – at school, for instance, or when a parent remarries and they inherit a stepsister. I have a story about this kind of mismatch – would you like to hear it?'

5

THE LITTLE PEOPLE

Penelope had begun to hate her stepsister. It had come upon her like a winter's night: suddenly the temperature just dropped. Now everything she felt about Laura was dark and cold.

It was true to say that Penelope had never really liked Laura, from the moment they met. When Penelope thought back to that day – when Laura and her mother first arrived at the house and her father had smiled like a fool and told her that she was to have a new mummy and a new sister – she felt physically sick.

Penelope hadn't wanted a new mother and she

certainly hadn't wanted a new sister. This wasn't because she felt an overriding love for or loyalty towards her deceased mother. She had never really loved her mother as she saw other children love theirs.

No. She resented these incomers because they spoiled everything. When her mother died, Penelope had had her father all to herself. And he was happier as a widower, she knew that. He seemed to have a lightness about him, and Penelope believed she had helped him to have it.

But now she realised that he was happier because he had met this woman: this awful, vain and pretentious creature who said she was an actress but was really some sort of artist's model – or 'muse', as she preferred to put it.

'Do you know that Rossetti said I had the most beautiful mouth he had ever seen?' said Penelope's stepmother with a pout.

Penelope did know this. In fact it must have been the fourth time she'd heard this particular piece of information. She also knew that Sir John Everett Millais had described her as 'a goddess' and had begged to be allowed to paint her portrait.

But as irritating as her stepmother was, she could not compete in Penelope's disaffection with her daughter, Laura.

Laura was very different from her mother. She had none of her mother's relentless hunger for the limelight, none of her mother's outlandishness of behaviour, but still she managed to attract more attention than Penelope.

In any event, Penelope found Laura's self-contained quietude even more odious than the shrill attention-seeking of her mother.

Penelope's father had already taken to calling Laura his 'little flower'. It jabbed Penelope like a needle every time she heard it. Her father had never called her anything but Penelope. He had not even shortened it to Penny as her mother had – not even once.

Laura's mother, and her contact – real or imagined – with these silly painters calling themselves the Pre-Raphaelite Brotherhood, seemed to have infected Laura and filled her head with all kinds of nonsense. She was forever singing silly songs about elfin knights and fairy queens, and Penelope would constantly find her reading poetry. She even gave a recital of John Keats' 'La Belle Dame Sans Merci' one evening after dinner.

'O what can ail thee, knight at arms,' she had intoned, dressed in a long white gown, 'Alone and palely loitering? The sedge has withered from the lake, And no birds sing . . .'

Penelope had yawned and sighed as much as she could before her stepmother hissed at her, but Laura could not be distracted. In fact Penelope believed that she had never intended to follow this poem with 'The Lady of Shalott' and only did so out of spite.

Penelope was not a lover of books or art or anything to speak of, and so was frequently bored. She was so bored that she would even have deigned to play with Laura, except that Laura never wanted to play anything at all.

Penelope would find Laura palely loitering around the house or the garden, her head in a book or else in the clouds. She was often talking to herself. Laura seemed to need no one else. She was utterly self-contained and self-reliant and Penelope hated her for it.

One day, as Penelope wandered aimlessly about the garden, she saw Laura standing under one of the old plum trees. She always had the suspicion that Laura posed herself in these picturesque locations on purpose.

The plum tree was heavy with white blossom,

the flowers full of busy bees. Laura was leaning against the green-grey lichen-covered trunk, threading daisies into a chain and talking to herself as usual. A small bird flitted away as Penelope approached.

'You do realise it's a sign of madness,' said Penelope, 'talking to yourself. You ought to watch out or else they'll cart you off to an asylum.'

Penelope allowed herself a moment to fully picture that delicious thought. Laura did not even bother to turn round. It was as if she had known Penelope was there.

'You'll end up in the crazy house,' said Penelope. 'Mark my words.'

'Mark my words' had been a favourite expression of her mother's, and Penelope found that she was using it more and more and rather liked the sound of it.

'Why do you hate me so much, I wonder?' said Laura, turning to face her at last.

There was something electric about the word 'hate' being out in the air between them.

'I don't hate you,' Penelope said unconvincingly. 'I don't even think about you at all.'

'Why do you follow me about then?' said Laura. 'If you do not think about me, why not leave me alone?'

It was true. Penelope did follow Laura about. She couldn't quite explain why she did so, and she found the question annoying.

'I can go where I like,' said Penelope. 'This is my house. This is my garden.'

'It is mine too,' said Laura. 'Like it or not.'

'Well, I do not,' said Penelope. 'I don't like it one little bit.'

'Well then,' said Laura with a giggle and a shrug. 'I don't see what I'm expected do about that.'

Penelope felt the colour rise to her cheeks. She hated the way she looked when that happened, which just made her all the more incensed.

'Everything was fine before you came!' she hissed.

Was she going to cry? Oh, how she hoped she would not cry. She couldn't bear the shame of crying in front of this awful creature.

'Your father seems happy enough with us here,' said Laura, bending down to pick another daisy.

Penelope wanted to kick her, to kick her in the face. Hard. More than once. But she controlled herself.

'At least I don't talk to myself,' she said.

'I wasn't talking to myself,' said Laura with a weary sigh. 'I was talking to . . .' Her voice trailed away.

'Talking to who?' said Penelope with a chuckle. 'You see – there was no one there.'

Laura gave her a withering look.

'I was talking to one of the little people,' she said after a short pause.

This was said with such bored matter-of-factness that Penelope was too dumbfounded to think of anything by way of reply that would do justice to so incredible a statement. Laura really was crazy.

'What nonsense are you saying now, Laura?' said Penelope.

Laura simply smiled and carried on threading daisies. Penelope's breathing sounded loud in her own ears; she wondered whether it sounded loud to Laura and she hoped it did not. But Laura's capacity to ignore her was so infuriating, some-times she really didn't know what she would do.

'You're saying that you have seen fairies?' said Penelope with a snort. 'Fairies? Do you realise how silly you sound? Do you realise how mad?'

Laura doggedly refused to speculate on her own silliness.

'Are you saying that you have seen fairies?' persisted Penelope, her face a picture of condescen-sion, her voice slightly scratchy.

'*You* might say so,' said Laura calmly, facing her

with a half-smile that Penelope had seen many times before and which she always found acutely annoying. Laura turned back to her daisies.

Penelope stared at the back of Laura's head, at the almost liquid sheen of her long auburn hair. She felt an almost uncontrollable urge to pick up the branch lying on the ground nearby and strike her with it. She even imagined the sound it would make as it cracked across Laura's skull. It was not an unpleasant sensation.

'Prove it, then,' said Penelope a little breathlessly, her heart still racing with the thought of punishing this irritating creature. 'Prove that you've seen these so-called fairies of yours.'

'I never called them fairies,' said Laura. 'You called them fairies.'

Penelope smiled. Laura was already beginning to back down.

'I said that I was talking to one of the little people when you saw me,' said Laura. 'And so I was. If you want to call them fairies, that is up to you.'

'These "little people",' said Penelope, sensing she had Laura on the run and placing as much disbelief as she could muster into her pronunciation of the words, 'are they just people who happen to be short – like my aunt Harriet? Because I had thought there was something special about them from the way you spoke. Oh – but, of course – they must be invisible too, mustn't they?'

Laura gave her a long hard look.

'They are not invisible.'

'Really?' said Penelope with a purse of her lips. 'Then why was it that I saw no one with you?'

'They are very shy,' said Laura. 'They flew away as you walked over.'

'Flew away?' said Penelope with a chuckle. 'They can fly, then? Are you sure they aren't fairies? They sound like fairies.'

'The little people are very special,' said Laura. 'But you wouldn't know anything about them. You're only interested in shopping. The little people know things you will never know.'

'Well, then,' said Penelope. 'If these "little people" are so special, I want to see them.'

Laura shook her head and gave Penelope a look of disbelief, raising her eyebrows as if the suggestion was the most preposterous thing she had ever heard.

'You can't see them.'

'I can't see them because they don't exist,' said Penelope triumphantly.

'You can't see them because they don't want to see you.'

'You are such an evil little liar,' said Penelope, jabbing her finger. 'Though it's hardly surprising, is it? Your mother's just the same.'

Laura gave her a long cold look that made Penelope step away, half fearing that Laura was about to attack.

'I really don't care if you believe me or not,' said Laura. 'Why should I care what you think? What possible reason would I have to care?'

Penelope stood squeezing her fingers into white-knuckled fists, her teeth clenched so tightly together she felt as though they might suddenly shatter under the pressure.

'Why don't they want to see me?' hissed Penelope. 'These stupid little people of yours.'

'They don't like you,' said Laura coolly.

Penelope scowled and took a step forward. She was troubled by how upset she was by this statement. It shouldn't matter what feelings Laura assigned to her imaginary creations, but for some reason it did.

'I'm sorry,' said Laura. 'But it's true. I don't know why they don't like you, but it's better to stay clear of them if they don't want you around.'

Had Penelope's stepmother not arrived at that moment to call Laura in for her piano lesson,

Penelope didn't know what she might have done. She was still shaking as she walked back to the house.

All Penelope's energy would now go into getting Laura to reveal what a foolish creature she was. She would watch her at every waking hour and force her to accept that her belief in these so-called 'little people' was a pathetic delusion. She would expose her as a fantasist to her father. Penelope knew that her father detested a liar above all things. She shivered with excitement at the shame and humiliation her stepsister was going to endure.

The much anticipated humiliation did not arrive, however. Though Penelope gave Laura every opportunity to talk about her little people at the supper table, she steadfastly refused to be drawn on the subject and it was Penelope who came away looking curiously obsessive about fairies.

The urge to make Laura look foolish took on a darker and darker shade as Penelope's hatred grew unchecked. She scarcely let Laura out of her sight. She had become fixated with this unrelenting need to catch her stepsister out.

She was determined that her father in particular should see Laura talking to her invisible friends.

But it wasn't easy to arrange. Every time Laura heard them coming – and she seemed to have the ears of a cat – she would pretend to be doing something else entirely.

Then, one day, Penelope saw Laura whispering away to herself by the pond and turned to see her father walking on the other side of the lawn. She couldn't believe her luck. Putting her finger to her lips, she beckoned him over.

'What is it, my dear?' he whispered as he joined her. 'Seen something, eh?' Her father was a keen amateur naturalist. 'Kingfisher, is it? I saw one myself the other day. Pretty thing.'

'No, Father,' whispered Penelope with a smirk. 'I wanted to show you –'

But just at that moment a huge dragonfly buzzed up in front of her face and she panicked, flapping wildly, and tumbled backwards into the pond. The water was not very deep and so Penelope was left sitting in a sorry state, enveloped in lily pads.

Laura came running at the sound of the splash, her face initially a picture of concern. But it was Penelope's father who was the first to break, his red face shuddering as he let out a trickle of giggles that turned into mighty guffaws, and his stepdaughter soon joined in enthusiastically. Penelope got to her feet and stomped away towards the house, deaf to her father's apologies and renewed guffawing.

This embarrassment did not dampen Penelope's urge to expose her stepsister; on the contrary. It concentrated the venom. Penelope would get her revenge if it took a year. She would wait and she would watch.

However, her renewed surveillance achieved nothing but yet more burning hatred fuelled by frustration. Penelope had caught Laura skulking about and occasionally talking to herself, but that was not enough. She still needed something that would show her father what his precious step-daughter was really like. But what?

Finally, one night, that opportunity arrived when Penelope heard a creaking floorboard outside her bedroom door and, on quietly opening it, saw Laura making her way furtively down the stairs. Astonished, Penelope heard the grating noise of the bolts on the outside door being drawn back.

Penelope grinned and went back into her room and across to the window. Was Laura really going out in the middle of the night? Yes – there she was, wandering out into the moonlight. She was crazier than Penelope had thought.

Penelope toyed with the idea of rousing her

father there and then and seeing how Laura would explain this eccentric behaviour.

But she did not. Though she couldn't allow herself to admit it, some tiny, hidden-away part of her wanted to believe that Laura might actually have contact with fairies.

Hastily putting on her robe, Penelope tiptoed down the hall and stairs and out of the house, walking barefoot across the lawn, the ground still warm from the heat of the day.

Moonlight washed across the scene, staining everything in its pale and dreamy glow – pale and dreamy, but bright enough to cast bold blue shadows across the lawn.

Laura was walking towards the garden gate, her white nightdress almost luminous in that eerie light. She looked more ghost than mortal child, flickering like a will-o'-the-wisp as she drifted into the murky shade of the copse.

Penelope followed her across the lawn as soon as she was in no danger of being seen should Laura turn and glance behind her. She could feel her heart beating with excitement as she wondered what to do next.

Should she shout out and rouse the household? Laura would have to explain what on earth she was doing wandering about the garden at midnight. But then so would Penelope.

She could see the figure of Laura glimmering ahead as she walked into the copse of oak and hazel trees that stood beyond the garden at the meadow's edge.

An owl hooted high in the trees above her and another replied from somewhere at the back of the house. Penelope looked up into the silhouetted branches and the owl hooted again. When she looked back, she saw that Laura had stopped.

Penelope crept forward inch by inch, denying herself even the quietest of winces when a bramble scratched across her bare ankle. Eventually she rested against the trunk of an oak and peered round at Laura and stared in open-mouthed astonishment. So incredible was the scene she was witnessing that her mind struggled to agree with the evidence of her eyes.

For there, quite plainly lit by the moonlight, was Laura, kneeling on the ground, her nightdress spread out on the grass of a little glade within the copse, and all about her – on the ground and flitting about her head – were dozens and dozens of tiny fairies.

These creatures seemed to have some kind of

supernatural luminescence and they glowed like fireflies, and each movement of their bodies increased the intensity of the glow until they shone like tiny stars. They flew back and forth in front of Laura's face and around her head, creating a kind of halo that shimmered with a beautiful blue-white light.

One of the fairy-folk seemed to spot Penelope and flitted towards Laura's shoulder. It whispered into Laura's ear and she turned slowly round.

Penelope stepped out from her hiding place and smiled expectantly, hoping that Laura would beckon her over to share the spell, but the expression on Laura's face was one of pure malice. Having given her a long stare so cold it made Penelope shiver, Laura turned away.

Penelope could see that Laura was speaking to the fairies, but could not hear her. The fairy-folk clustered around her in the air, hanging on to her nightdress and sitting on her shoulders. More and more appeared from the darkness; there must have been hundreds of them now.

Penelope watched in anticipation as, once again, Laura turned to face her, and a bright mass of little faces did likewise. Then Laura's mouth moved in a tight-lipped whisper and there was a soft rustling as all of the fairies took to their wings and hovered in a swarm before moving towards Penelope.

Penelope was slow to react, still mesmerised by the beauty of these magical creatures and the wonderful glow that emanated from the cluster as they flew.

It was not until they were hovering only a few feet away from her face that she actually saw them for what they were; only then did she see their faces clearly, their terrible, black and twinkling eyes, their scabrous flesh, their grinning mouths, their vicious teeth and grasping claws.

Penelope opened her mouth to scream, but the swarm was on her in a heartbeat.

Penelope's stepmother found her in the morning when she went for her morning commune with nature. She was entangled in a coil of brambles, her pale flesh scribbled with scratches, her eyes wide open in panic.

The cause of death could not be determined. The doctor surmised that Penelope had walked in her sleep, become ensnared in the bushes and the ensuing panic had resulted in a heart attack. Some people's hearts were weaker than others, he explained.

It was all very tragic, but Penelope's stepmother rather enjoyed tragedy. She certainly took to organising the funeral with enthusiasm, and everyone agreed it was a most moving and beautiful service. Laura read a poem of her own creation.

It was about fairies.

The image of that swarm of devilish little creatures seemed reluctant to leave my mind. Again I had a dreamlike vision of the scene, and again that same strange impression that there was someone or something else away in the shadows that had not been mentioned in the tale.

I was so distracted by my efforts to discern what this might be before the vision's inevitable dissolution that I think the Woman in White may have spoken to me more than once before I finally replied.

'Hello?' I answered, rather stupidly. 'Sorry, yes – I was . . .'

I didn't quite know where that sentence was destined to go and so I let it die partway between us. My brain was begging for the comfort of sleep. I shook my head drowsily.

'You seem troubled,' said the Woman in White, but in a way that did not quite speak of concern. It was as if she were interested and intrigued by my every action. She patently seemed to regard any discomfort caused by her tales as a kind of achievement, though I could not begrudge her that. Were I to tell a tale like that, I should want to trouble my listener a little. After all, that was half the fun.

'No,' I said. 'Not troubled, exactly. The story was rather strange. Had I heard it as a bedtime story, it would probably have disturbed my sleep. But luckily I do not believe in fairies – vicious ones or otherwise.'

'Of course,' she said. 'You're a rationalist, as we have established.'

'I suppose I am. I don't know.'

'You seek a rational explanation for the world.'

'Nevertheless, I enjoy stories of a supernatural sort,' I said. 'But I know they are just stories. I don't think such things truly exist in the real world. Sometimes I wish they did.' I smiled and then added, 'Though I am happy to do without murderous fairies.'

'The real world?' she said in a questioning tone.

'Yes,' I said, not fully understanding how there could be any confusion. 'This world.' I waved my hands about to encompass the carriage, the train, the cutting and beyond. 'Our world.'

The Woman in White smiled her strange smile, eyes glittering.

'Have you never had any hint, then, that there might be more to this world than there appears?'

'I've never seen fairies, I know that,' I said with a smile. 'I think I should have remembered if I had.'

'Your stepmother is of a rather different opinion regarding these things, though, isn't that true?'

Again, the conversation seemed to have returned to my stepmother.

'Undoubtedly,' I said. 'She is entitled to her opinion. I think she is mistaken, however.'

The Woman in White cocked her head, studying me intently.

'Do you not think it odd that your stepmother had a vision of a tunnel and here we are?'

I had no recollection of telling her the content of my stepmother's vision. My mind really was becoming quite addled.

'Yes,' I said. 'I suppose that it is odd. She did see a tunnel. But then she also saw . . .'

I remembered my stepmother's premonition of a kiss and blushed. It felt unseemly to mention it to this young woman whom I barely knew.

'Yes?' said the Woman in White with a raised eyebrow.

'That's the point, isn't it,' I said, changing the subject with a cough. 'There will always be coincidences, and those who wish to see some significance in them will do so. There are tunnels on this line and my stepmother and everyone else knows it. In any event, my stepmother foresaw danger, and while this interruption in our journey is tedious in the extreme, it is hardly dangerous.'

'Ah,' said the Woman in White. 'But your journey is not over yet.'

She said these words in the same prim and proper way she said everything else, but there was an edge to them somehow.

I turned to look at my fellow passengers, once more willing them to wake, and when that failed I coughed loudly, but to no effect. The Farmer's hands twitched a little, that was all.

'All travel is fraught with danger,' said the Woman in White.

'We are only travelling to London,' I said witheringly. 'We are not trying to find the North-West Passage.'

She smiled at my sarcasm, and I have to say I was quite pleased by the quickness of my response.

'You have not travelled much,' she said, making it sound more of a statement than a question.

'No,' I said. 'I've never left the British Isles. In fact, come to think of it, I have never actually left England.'

This realisation made me rather depressed. England was a very fine place and surely the best country in the whole world; but even so, it would have been nice to test this theory by going somewhere else.

'Scotland is a most Romantic place,' she said. 'Have you never wished to travel there?'

'I can't say I have,' I replied.

'I have a story about one of the islands of that country,' she said, in total disregard to my stated lack of interest. 'Would you like to hear it?'

'Well . . .' I began.

'Excellent,' she said.

6

THE CROTACH STONE

The Western Isles of Scotland must have seemed like the edge of the world to our ancient ancestors as they moved ever northwards against the retreating ice. Even with our knowledge of the world as a circumnavigated globe, these islands can still seem as if they stand sentinel at the ends of the earth.

It was along a bumpy track on the western shore of one such island that a pony and cart made its tortuous way, an inconsequential dot against the wide expanse of moor, of dune, of sand and sea. A small group of houses was visible a couple of miles or so ahead on the shore of an inlet, huddled round a squat church.

Dr Fraser winced as the wheel of the cart he had insisted on driving himself juddered over yet another pothole. Davy turned away from his father and looked out over the wide bay of bone-white sand with blue-black mountains beyond, their summits wigged with woollen clouds. His father pulled the reins and called to the pony to stop, which it happily did, immediately turning its great head to munch at some grass.

'We'll take a wee walk,' he said to his son. 'Stretch our legs, eh?'

'But won't we be late?' said Davy sulkily.

'Come on,' said his father. 'I think we can spare a few moments to look at the view.'

Dr Fraser climbed down and Davy followed him over a low stone wall, his father rhapsodising about everything that came into view, from the wild flowers to the cloud-covered hilltops in the distance. Davy said little in response.

They crossed a patch of hummocky grass, close-cropped by rabbits whose burrows could be seen to the right and left as they climbed to the top of a mountainous sand dune and looked out over the wide Atlantic.

'Nothing like this in Edinburgh, eh, Davy boy?'

Davy said nothing. What was there to say? Of course there was nothing like this in Edinburgh, just as there was nothing like Edinburgh in this empty wasteland.

But he had to admit it was dramatic. Even though it was a sunny day, the wind and sea roared so loudly that it blocked out most other noise, save for the hoarse shrieks of seabirds. Davy's father had to shout to make himself heard.

'What a place!' he called. 'What an extraordinary place!'

Davy still made no reply. His father's smile slowly faded and he turned to walk down a cleft in the dune towards the beach. Davy let him get fifty yards ahead before he followed him.

Davy understood that his father had not been happy in Edinburgh since Davy's mother had died. He understood that his father wanted a new challenge to occupy his grieving mind. But understanding did not make Davy forgive this move away from friends: away from the city he had grown up in, away from his mother's grave in Greyfriars. A move to the Outer Hebrides was a move to a world of barren nothingness.

The Outer Hebrides: even the name had something mournful and final about it, like the name of some remote destination in a Greek myth or Norse saga. It sounded like a place people were banished to or washed up on.

They were building a great herring-packing site and Davy's father was to be employed as doctor to the workers and to the rest of the population. But Davy found it hard to marry the idea of a modern fishery with this backward place. He would be less surprised to see a Viking ship round the headland than he would a steamer.

This impression was only compounded when Davy and his father noticed a tall stone stabbed into the top of the nearby dunes like Excalibur. As they walked towards it, the sunlight shifted theatrically, a spotlight beam rushing over the tussocks and lighting the stone as if it were an actor on a stage.

The stone was very tall – Davy thought it must be well over seven feet – and bent over. There was something human about the way it seemed to lean into the wind. Davy had the disconcerting feeling that were he to tap it, the stone would turn to face him.

He could see that the stone was a long block of granite or some such, salmon pink and grey, with quartz crystals twinkling here and there, though there was little of the rock visible. It was covered in all kinds of lichen: pale blue-grey, white, blotches of egg-yolk yellow and light seaweed-like tufts; the whole thing looked like a stone one might find at the bottom of a rock pool, hauled up and set on end to dry in the incessant wind.

There were bird droppings on the top and dripping down the sides, and fragments of mussel shells at the foot.

'A bird has been using this as an anvil,' said his father with a smile. 'They break the shells to get at the food.'

Davy nodded absent-mindedly. His father had spent his boyhood on the island of Mull and was always trying to interest Davy in the natural world – a world in which Davy had not the slightest interest whatsoever. He longed for the smoke-blackened walls and cobbled streets of Edinburgh.

Davy's attention moved to the ground on the other side of the stone, for there were more things there than just pieces of shell. He crouched down for a better look.

Half hidden in the tussocks of grass was another stone set into the ground. It had a cleft in it and stuffed into this gap was a strange collection of objects. Davy's father had come round and also noticed the things at the stone's base.

A brass candlestick glinted in the sunlight next to a piece of lace; a silver spoon lay next to those, and behind them Davy could also see a book, something that may have been a hat pin, a silk scarf, a brooch and various other items of jewellery.

'You there!' shouted a man some way off, standing on the track. 'Come away!'

Davy stood up straight away and saw his father bristle at the manner of this address, but like Davy, he had seen that the man was carrying a shotgun and was pointing it in their direction.

'Come on, Davy,' said his father hoarsely.

They walked back across the grass towards the man with the gun. He did not lower it until they had scaled the small drystone wall and were back on the track.

'I do not take kindly to having a gun pointed at me,' said Dr Fraser, frowning at the stranger. 'Nor at my son.'

'You have no right to be on that ground,' said the man, who Davy could now see was old, grey hair peeping out from under his cap. His nose was red and had the look of worn leather about it. He was quite the most unfriendly-looking person Davy had ever met.

'I apologise if we've done something wrong,' said Dr Fraser. 'We are new to the island. But still we –'

'Stay away from here,' he growled. 'You have no business on the dunes.'

'But I am the new doc–' began Davy's father, but the old man sniffed and walked on.

'How extraordinary!' said Dr Fraser. 'What a spectacularly ill-mannered creature.' He chuckled and shook his head. 'Let's hope they're not all like that, eh?'

'I wish I was in Edinburgh!' hissed Davy.

Davy's father sighed, and looked from his son's down-turned face to the standing stone silhouetted against the sea.

'Aye, well, we're here and that's that,' he said. 'Come on. Mr McLeod will be wondering what's become of us.'

He turned and walked back to the pony and cart, and after a moment's hesitation, Davy followed him. The wind blew at his back and all at once it seemed to carry on its breath the sound of whispers. Davy turned round, but there was nothing to see but the dunes and the stone.

It wasn't long before Davy and his father arrived at the house that was to be their home for the foreseeable future. As they climbed down from the cart and walked up the path, Davy turned and, looking back, could still make out the stone on the horizon.

The house was considerably grander than most of the houses round about, and a palace in comparison to the low, turf-topped crofts they had passed en route from the harbour.

'Dr Fraser, I presume?' called the wiry, weather-beaten man who stood at the front steps.

'Aye,' said Dr Fraser, shaking his hand. 'And you must be Mr McLeod.'

'At your service, Doctor,' he said. 'Come away inside.'

They walked through the stone-flagged hall into the parlour, and McLeod introduced his mother.

Davy hadn't even noticed the old woman sitting wrapped in a shawl by the fire when he'd entered the room. She looked like an owl, slightly startled by the intrusion.

'Mrs McLeod,' said Dr Fraser.

The old woman smiled and nodded.

'This fine-looking lad must be your son,' said McLeod.

'Shake hands, Davy,' said his father. 'Where are your manners?'

Davy held out his hand and McLeod shook it warmly.

'I trust the crossing was not too rough,' he said, looking at Davy's sour expression.

'Not at all, Mr McLeod,' said Dr Fraser. 'The sea was as calm as a mill pond.'

'Well now,' he said. 'That's a blessing. And your journey here?'

'Aye,' said Dr Fraser. 'We had a little meeting with one of the locals. Not an especially friendly one.'

'Is that so?' said McLeod, his smile fading. 'Well, I'm sorry to hear that.'

Dr Fraser explained what had happened and McLeod listened intently, nodding all the while and sighing every now and then.

'That will be Murdo,' said McLeod.

'He looks after the auld folk,' said Mrs McLeod. 'He's a good man.'

'I hadn't wished to suggest he wasn't, madam,' said Dr Fraser with a smile.

'He can be – how shall we put it now? – lacking in the social graces,' said McLeod. 'But he means no harm.'

'I'm sure he's a fine fellow. He told us in parting to stay away from the dunes,' said Dr Fraser. 'We were just looking at the old standing stone there.'

McLeod took a deep breath and put his hands together as if in prayer. Davy saw him cast a nervous glance towards his mother, but the old lady stayed silent.

'That would be the Clach Crotach,' he said.

'I beg your pardon?' said Dr Fraser.

'Do you not have the Gaelic, Doctor?' said McLeod.

'A long time ago, aye, when I was a lad,' Davy's father replied sadly. 'I'm hoping it will come back while I'm here.'

'Well, that would be grand, wouldn't it?' said McLeod. 'Clach means stone. Crotach means, well, hunchbacked. The Hunchback Stone.'

'But why was this man Murdo so incensed at us being there?' said Dr Fraser.

McLeod looked uncomfortable. Davy could sense a nervousness in him; his father sensed it too.

'The Crotach Stone is from the days before the Word of the Gospels reached the island, Dr Fraser,' said McLeod after a pause.

'Aye?' said Dr Fraser. 'Well then. I'm surprised to see that sort of thing still standing here. I had heard that the people of these islands were God-fearing folk. Can you not strike it down, Mr McLeod?'

McLeod's eyes widened a little.

'Strike it down?' he echoed quietly, almost to himself.

'Aye, man,' said Dr Fraser. 'I reckon you and your sons –'

'I could not do that, Doctor,' said McLeod emphatically.

'Och, the auld folk would not like that,' said Mrs McLeod. 'They wouldn't like that at all.'

'Hush now, Mother,' said McLeod.

'But surely –' began Dr Fraser.

'You're new to the islands, Doctor,' said McLeod as if he had suddenly realised he was only talking to a child. 'We do not take kindly to change. If you're to get on here, it would be best to understand that.'

Though it was said with a smile, Davy felt there was the hint of a threat in McLeod's tone of voice.

'There were objects near that stone,' said Dr Fraser. 'Valuable objects, some of them. I hope that the people hereabouts are not in thrall to that heathen thing.'

McLeod smiled.

'Och now, Dr Fraser,' he said. 'Do not sound so shocked and put out. Some folk leave offerings at the Stone, that is all.'

'Good Lord. For what purpose?' asked Davy's father, frowning.

McLeod shrugged.

'Och, you know the kind of thing,' he said, as if leaving offerings at a standing stone were the most natural thing in the world. 'They are going across the water to the mainland and want a safe journey; their daughter is having a baby and they want her to have a happy labour . . .'

Davy saw his father bristle slightly.

'There are those who do continue to follow the auld ways,' McLeod explained. 'We are simple folk here, Doctor. You must forgive us our eccentricities. I'm sure the people of Edinburgh are far too sophisticated for such things.'

'You must have respect for the auld folk,' said Mrs McLeod.

'Mother, please . . .' said McLeod. 'Dr Fraser, I beg you not to think too harshly of the folk hereabout. They are good people, I promise you. You'll not find more God-fearing souls in all of Scotland.'

Dr Fraser took a deep breath and looked at his son.

'Will you not have a dram with me, sir,' said McLeod. 'I often find things seem less shocking after a dram.'

Dr Fraser smiled despite himself and put his hand to his forehead, rubbing it gently.

'Aye, Mr McLeod,' he said. 'A dram would be very welcome.'

McLeod went into another room and returned with a bottle of malt whisky and two small glasses, together with a pot of tea and two cups and saucers.

'I took the liberty of having a bottle brought to the house,' said McLeod. 'I hope that was all right?'

'It is very kind of you. Will you not join us, Mrs McLeod?' asked Dr Fraser.

'Och, no, Doctor,' said McLeod. 'Mother does not drink. Do you, Mother?'

'What's that?' said Mrs McLeod. She turned to Davy and smiled. 'You're a good boy, aren't you? You'll mind the auld folk, won't you now, eh? You'll leave them be, won't you?'

'Aye,' said Davy, not seeing what else he could say. If the 'auld folk' of the island were all like Mrs McLeod, leaving them be would be no hardship. McLeod handed him a cup of tea.

'There's a good lad,' said Mrs McLeod. 'He's a good boy, Alasdair. A fine boy.'

'Hush now, Mother,' said McLeod. 'You're embarrassing the poor lad. Slaandjivaa, Doctor.'

'Slaandjivaa,' said Dr Fraser, raising his glass. 'That's a fine drop of whisky.'

131

The two men talked and Davy drifted away in his imagination to the streets of Edinburgh and to their old life there. He was brought back to the present by the sound of his father putting his glass on the table with a clink.

'Tell me more about the people hereabouts, Mr McLeod,' said Dr Fraser. 'I am keen to hear more about my patients and their superstitious ways.'

'Why, Doctor,' said McLeod, 'when you have lived here a wee while you might understand why it is that people still have a bond with the water, the sea and the weather . . .'

'And a pagan stone,' said Dr Fraser with a raise of his eyebrow.

'Aye, well,' said McLeod. 'On that subject, I'm afraid I must ask you to stay away from that particular part of the island. And young Davy there as well, of course.'

'Or shall we be shot?' said Dr Fraser with a grin. 'Will old Murdo come after us with a shotgun?'

McLeod sighed deeply and smiled wearily.

'Don't be too hasty to make judgements, Dr Fraser,' he said. 'We are all very grateful for the new laird and his fishery and for the employment it will give the young men of the island, but this is not the mainland, Doctor. We are not so quick to brush away our heritage and our traditions here.'

'I didn't mean to give any offence, Mr McLeod,' said Davy's father quietly, clearly wishing he had not been so eager to tease. 'The whisky has loosened my tongue and my manners. Forgive me.'

McLeod smiled and said that there was nothing to forgive and that he was sure they would all get along famously, given time. He poured them both another drink.

'The Stone is important to the folk here,' he went on. 'I couldn't really explain it fully to someone like yourself who has never lived here. It is something you just grow up with on the island.'

'What are you telling them now, Alasdair?' said McLeod's mother, frowning.

'Nothing to concern you, Mother.'

'Alasdair's a good boy,' she said, looking at Davy and then his father. 'He's always been good to the auld folk.'

'Mother,' said McLeod with a smile and a shake of the head. 'Hush now.'

He turned to Dr Fraser and dropped his voice.

'I'm sorry for Mother,' he said. 'She does not always know what is going on these days.'

'I understand,' said Davy's father. 'There's no need to apologise. You were telling us about the Stone.'

'Och, there's nothing more to say really,' said McLeod, putting his glass down. 'But I must ask you to humour us in this matter and stay clear of the dunes and the Stone.'

There was a change in McLeod's manner as he spoke. Davy was aware of a new earnestness in the man's voice, almost as if he were warning them of something. His mind went back to Murdo – the man with the shotgun.

These people are crazy, Davy thought, *crazy enough to shoot a person for walking on a patch of ground they think is special for some stupid reason.*

'And another thing,' said McLeod with a rather forced smile. 'Should you be tempted to go round the dunes on to the beach beyond, be aware that the tide comes in awful quick there and the current is fearful strong. It's best avoided altogether.'

With that, McLeod got to his feet and smiled, rubbing his hands together, and said that it was time he and his mother left them in peace. If there was anything they needed – anything at all – they had only to ask. His house was just a quarter of a mile away.

The following weeks dragged slowly by for Davy. He looked forward to the end of the holidays when he would return to the mainland to go to school, although even that was not without its negative aspects, for it was a new school and Davy did not make friends easily. In fact, at his last school, he had not made friends at all.

His father's enthusiasm for the island was infuriating. The more boring Davy found it to be, the more his father would trumpet the discovery of some new bay or hill or patch of peat bog.

And if the days were dull, then the nights were interminable. The island was further north than Edinburgh and so the summer days seemed to stretch on for ever, as a strange twilight lit the land at ten o'clock at night.

Davy had difficulty sleeping and resented the fact that there was this gift of extra daylight hours without the least use to put it to. And even if there had been anything to amuse him, he wouldn't have been given the opportunity to make use of it, because his father still insisted on enforcing his bedtime.

Many a night Davy would lie awake, staring at the ceiling, staring at the curtained window and the glow that lit its floral pattern, seething with resentment, fuming with anger at his father for bringing them to this godforsaken place.

It was on one such twilit night that Davy got up from his bed, unable to sleep, and went to the window. Pulling back the curtains, he looked out over the bay, the sea a strange mother-of-pearl hue, more like burnished metal than water.

There was something so unearthly about that daylight that was not quite daylight; it gave everything an ominous look.

His attention moved to the Clach Crotach – the Hunchback Stone – and its forbidden dunes. An idea suddenly occurred to Davy and he smiled. Why had he not thought of it before?

The next day could not have been more different to the eerie stillness of the previous night. The Atlantic Ocean was wild and flecked with white foam. Brooding clouds capped the far hills and a fierce wind whistled round the eaves of the house and bullied the few twisted trees that stood about it.

Davy set off along the track as soon as breakfast was over and his father had left for the fisheries. Dr Fraser had grinned happily when Davy had told him that he intended to go for a run. *At last the boy seems to be accepting this place a little,* he thought. *At last he seems to have stopped moping about.*

Davy walked a short way up the track before running away from the house and away from town and past the Hunchback Stone. After about a mile he turned off on to a narrow path that led down to the shore.

He ran between two dunes, his feet sinking in the soft sand, the dune grass whistling in the wind. He ran on to the open white sand that stretched out in a kind of dreamlike blankness in all directions, and on, crossing the tideline, shells and dried seaweed crunching and crackling underfoot, until he reached the water's edge. The sea roared and growled deafeningly as he stood hands on hips, doubled over, panting.

The cloud was so low it moved across the bay like a sea fret, shrouding the far hills and mountains of the mainland, so visible on clear days.

This concealing veil emboldened Davy. He was in an enclosed world, shielded by the mist and by the raucous music of the weather. No one could see or hear him, that was for sure.

He approached the Crotach Stone, though something about the strange horizonless view and the swirling mist made it seem as though the Stone approached him, looming darkly.

Davy looked at the offerings at the foot of the

Stone: the offerings he was about to steal. There was nothing he really wanted. The aim was to cause as much offence to these awful people – to Mrs McLeod and the other 'auld folk' of this wretched place – as he could.

It would be obvious who had taken them. No one else on that pathetic island would ever have had the gumption to do it. They would know it was Davy and the shame and scandal would be too great to bear. His father would never be able to stay. They would be shunned and spurned. They would be lucky to leave with their lives once old shotgun-wielding Murdo heard about it. But at least they would leave, and that was all Davy cared about.

He pushed his hand into the cleft. He rooted around and suddenly winced, pulling his hand free. There was a gash in his forefinger. It was deep and opened horribly as he looked at it, the slippery pink workings under his ripped skin all too visible. Davy felt queasy and reached out to hold the Stone for support. It was surprisingly warm to the touch.

Blood dripped in great ruby drops, falling on to the cleft rock and the lace handkerchief and the candlestick and the carving knife deep down that had given him the wound. He grabbed the handkerchief and wrapped it round his fingers. It was wet from the mist and salty, but it was better than nothing.

Davy looked at the drips of blood on the cleft stone and grinned to himself. *What could be more valuable than your own blood?* he thought. If that did not merit a wish, then what would?

'I wish Father would grow to loathe this place as I do,' snarled Davy bitterly. 'I wish he would take me back to Edinburgh and be done with this stinking island.'

Once the wish was made, Davy felt a little foolish. It was all well and good to make a wish, but he was not as gullible as Mrs McLeod and the rest of the 'auld folk' of this backward place. He grabbed a few of the more portable objects – an old watch, a spoon, a snuffbox, a brooch – and stuffed them in his pockets. He stood up and walked away, heading down towards the beach, so that he could circle back unseen.

He looked back at the Crotach Stone on the dune top and his heart fluttered. There was something about it that really did suggest a man – a hunchbacked man – standing, leaning forward into the breeze, waiting, listening.

Davy turned away and then looked back quickly. He laughed to himself. Was he really trying to trick the Stone into giving itself away? He had definitely been on the island too long. He laughed again as he stared at the Stone. But it was a nervous laugh, and when he walked away he did not look back a third time.

His finger was throbbing and the lace handkerchief was wine red. He wanted to unwrap it to check his finger but he could not bring himself to do it. He walked over to the dune, his head spinning a little.

'I hate this place!' Davy yelled into the indifferent roar of the wind. 'I HATE THIS PLACE!'

As he walked towards the beach, he noticed for the first time that there were signs of old buildings embedded in the dunes. Walls formed from great hunks of salmon-pink and sea-green granite lay peeping from beneath a blanket of sand, veins of quartz glittering wetly.

Davy sat down with his back to a dune so tall it could have sheltered an army. He rested in an oasis of calm amid the savage roar of the wind, the ocean growling and snarling and frothing rabidly below him at the sand's end.

He took a deep breath, and the smell of the salt air and the heady scent of seaweed pulped by the breakers on the shore stung his nostrils. The wind had found a tiny gap in the dune's defences and was swirling the sand into a spinning vortex of sugary grains. As they spun, they lifted the sand to reveal something buried beneath.

Davy leaned forward to give the wind a helping hand, curious to see what this sunken thing might be. Two or three passes of his bloodied, bandaged hand revealed, to his horror, a face: a human face, very pale, its eyes closed as in sleep.

Davy scrabbled back, staring wide-eyed at the face, the sand shifting about its nose and brow and pallid, white forehead. It was a body buried in the sand.

He thought of the warning to stay away and wondered with dread if he was looking at the body of the last person who did not heed that warning.

He made himself creep back closer and bent forward, fascinated. It couldn't have been here for long. There was no sign of decomposition.

Then the eyes opened and Davy screamed.

He stood up to run away but as he turned he saw three or four more faces rising out of the fine white sand, like sleepers awakening from a deep slumber. He stopped, too shocked to know what to do other than yell.

'Father!' he shouted. 'Father!'

But the wind took his words and sent them fluttering out across the sand.

Something grabbed his leg. Davy looked down and saw an arm emerging out of the sand near his feet and holding his shin. He tried to shake it off but the arm was stronger and began to pull him down.

The last thing Davy saw was the Crotach Stone standing on the dunes above him, leaning into the mist, as the wind screamed in his ears. The auld folk crowded in around him and the sand flooded over him like water.

'Will you be wanting a funeral, Doctor?' said McLeod. 'I know the man to speak to. If you want me to see him, I will.'

'No,' said Dr Fraser coldly. 'That will not be necessary, thank you. I think it would be proper to take Davy back to Edinburgh. His mother is . . .' His voice faded away.

'Aye,' said McLeod. 'I understand.'

Dr Fraser had Davy's body packed in salt by the foreman at the fishery, and two days later he was ready to sail back to Edinburgh. He would bury Davy next to his mother in Greyfriars Cemetery.

As the cart pulled away from the house, Dr

Fraser's eyes were drawn irresistibly to the standing stone on the dune top. A passing cloud had plunged that area into deep shadow while the sea beyond was dazzling bright with sunlight.

The Clach Crotach stood black against the brightness like an exclamation mark, and the doctor's mind unwillingly returned to the scene at the beach where they'd found him – Davy's body on the shoreline, lying tangled in seaweed, his flesh horribly savaged by the action of sea and sand.

What had possessed the boy to swim in the sea on a day like that? Why could he not have heeded McLeod's warning about the tide?

Dr Fraser turned his collar against the cold wind that suddenly seemed to be blowing up from the west, tossing the manes of the horses and fluttering the canvas lain across his son's coffin. He wanted nothing more than to get away. He had never loathed anything so much as he loathed that island now.

Again the image was so very clear in my mind: the Crotach Stone, the fearful 'auld folk', the remains of Davy left on the tideline like driftwood. And again there was that other something in the lee of the giant dune. But as before, the image slipped away before I could discern what it was.

I had always had something of a prejudice against the Scottish islands, and this tale had done nothing to dispel it. There was a boy from those parts in my dorm at school and he was the most frightful bore. He never missed an opportunity to regale us with the supposed wonders of the islands. I resolved in that instant never to be tempted to travel north.

'Do you believe the past can live on and affect the present?' asked the Woman in White.

'I suppose I do in a way,' I said, leaning back in my seat. 'I mean to say, history is deuced important. But I don't think that it can actually *live* on. I mean, I don't believe in ghouls that can rise up and grab you. I don't believe in ghosts. I do not believe in the supernatural at all.'

'No?' she said, with raised eyebrows.

'No,' I said.

She sat looking at me with a curious expression midway between amusement and disbelief. I found it intensely annoying and make no apologies for the fact that I frowned back at her in response. After all, this woman barely knew me. What cause had she to doubt anything I told her? I did not believe in the supernatural and that was an end to it.

I thought that people who claimed to believe in such things were charlatans or, at best, misguided or mistaken in some way. I was sure that most so-called supernatural occurrences could be explained, provided a sufficiently rational mind was brought to bear. Had I been a witness to something I couldn't explain, perhaps I would have felt differently, but I had not.

But then . . . there was one curious incident when I was very small that came back to me in that carriage, came back to me with a startling vividness.

'What is it?' said the Woman in White.

I was about to say that it was nothing, but I found that I had an urge to tell this story before it faded once again.

'I was remembering something,' I said. 'Something I had forgotten – or thought I had forgotten.'

'Yes?' she said.

'I was playing near the river not far from our home. I was young: not more than five years old. I slipped and plunged into the water. Although I was able to swim a little, the water was cold and deep and full of eddies and underwater weeds in which I quickly became entangled.

'I cried out, but that just meant I swallowed a mouthful of foul-tasting water and began to sink even further among the reeds. I tried with all my might to make for the riverbank, but to no avail.

'Then a woman who must have been walking nearby came to my aid. She leaned down and reached out to me. I stretched out my arm to meet hers, but the gap between our fingers, though it could hardly have been more than a few inches, might as well have been a mile.

'I cried out again and splashed even more desperately, but if anything the gap seemed to get bigger. My vision was blurred by the water in my eyes and by my own tears, and I could see nothing clearly at all except the fingers of the woman's hands.

'She leaned so far over the edge of the riverbank that she was in real danger of falling in herself. But still our fingers didn't meet and I continued to flounder in the cold river.

'All my hope drained away. I seemed doomed to drown, and the poor woman who would have been my rescuer likewise doomed to watch it happen. There was no time for her to go for help. Had she done so I would have been at the bottom of the river before she found anyone.

'Then suddenly there was a great splash and I felt strong arms around me and I was lifted free of the weeds and pulled clear of the river and out on to the bank, where I lay coughing and spluttering in the arms of my father.

'My mother was there at his side, crying and calling my name and stroking my hair. My father was crying as well. It was the first and last time I ever saw him do so. And, to complete the picture, I too was overcome with sobbing, so grateful was I to have been saved.

'I looked in vain for the woman who had tried to save me, but there was no one there. I asked my parents where she'd gone, for they couldn't have failed to see her: she was there only an instant before they arrived. But they said they'd seen no one and when they asked me what she looked like, I found that I could give them only the very vaguest description: the more I tried to fix her image in my mind, the more it slipped away, like a dream does when you wake up.

'My mother was convinced that it must have been my guardian angel, trying to give me hope until help arrived.'

'And what do you believe?' said the Woman in White.

'I don't know,' I said. 'It was a long time ago. But she had certainly helped me. Without the woman on the riverbank holding out her hand to me, I may have given myself up to the river.'

'And yet still you are resistant to the notion of the supernatural,' she said with a smile.

'I may simply have imagined it,' I said. 'Or the woman may have walked away and my parents, too preoccupied by my rescue, failed to notice her.'

The Woman in White clasped her hands together and shook her head.

'Always looking for a rational explanation,' she said.

'Is that so very bad?' I asked.

'Sometimes the rational is no defence against the irrational.'

'Yes, but we're only talking about stories,' I said. 'Mr Wells can write about monsters from Mars, after all – but that doesn't mean they exist.'

'It doesn't mean they do not,' she answered.

'I'm sorry,' I said with a frown. 'I don't follow you.'

'Just because something is told as a story and that story is part legend or myth, or feat of imagination, does not mean there is no truth in it.'

'Well, no,' I said, 'I suppose . . .'

'But why don't I tell you another story?' she said. 'I may as well. There is very little else to entertain us.'

I looked around at the sleepers in the compartment and was forced to agree with her.

'Very well,' I said. 'What is the story going to be about?'

'Oh, but that would spoil it entirely,' she said with a grin.

7

GERALD

Emma Reynolds clumped up the steep cobbled street, a few yards behind her mother. The stones were slippery from the morning's rain and the wet street had a snakeskin sheen to it.

'Do come along, Emma darling,' said her mother, pausing for a moment to give her daughter a look of undisguised disappointment and pity. 'And please do not stare at the ground when you walk. You know how much it vexes me. Upright back, upright soul. That's what Mr Cartwright says. Come along.'

Emma didn't reply. Mr Cartwright was the

minister and Emma's mother was fond of quoting him. Emma had a sneaking suspicion that her mother was a tiny bit in love with Mr Cartwright, and she smiled guiltily at the thought.

They reached the summit of the hill and a rather red-faced Emma let out a long gasp, which produced yet another disparaging look from her mother.

'You really must begin to think of yourself as a young lady, Emma,' she said. 'And start to behave like one.'

'Yes, Mother,' said Emma in weary response.

They made their way through the town, Mrs Reynolds saying good morning to everyone they met, much to Emma's embarrassment, and eventually ended up at the marketplace. The stalls glowed with colour between ranks of people dressed as dourly as the grey buildings that enclosed the square and the drab sky that hung above them.

Emma noticed that there was a cluster of children at one corner of the market, outside the Corn Exchange. There were so many children, and so many adults with them, that it was impossible to see what it was that they were looking at, save for a glimpse of red and yellow awning.

Emma's mother fell into conversation with

Mr Gilbertson from the library, concerning the scandalous behaviour of someone Emma did not know. She found her mother's gossiping tedious in the extreme and pleaded to be allowed to join the other children.

Permission gained, within moments Emma had squeezed her way among the crowd standing at the edge of the marketplace beside the low, spiked iron railings of the Corn Exchange. She watched, spellbound.

Everything around her – the incessant chatter and prattle of the town square – seemed to recede, to fall away, to drift from her consciousness. It was a puppet show and oh, how Emma loved a puppet show.

She pushed herself forward through the crowd, ignoring the grumbles of other children and admonishing tuts from their parents. Emma only had eyes and ears for the puppet show dazzling and shining before her like some kind of jewel in that dull, grey northern town.

A cold gust of wind blew in occasionally from the moors, but Emma did not feel it. She warmed herself in front of the brightly coloured little theatre stall as surely as if it had been a brazier full of burning coals.

The show exceeded her expectations, the puppets moving with a grace that Emma admired all the more for knowing that she would never share it.

The costumes were exquisite, making the dainty puppets look like the most delicate of tropical birds or brilliantly coloured insects. It was like a dream, a lovely, lovely dream.

Emma's mother tried several times to tug her away, but it would have taken a carthorse to pull her, and Mrs Reynolds was a petite and rather spindly woman. So she gave up and said she would return for Emma in ten minutes and that she was to come then, no matter what was happening in the silly show.

But Emma was not even listening to her. Why would she listen to her mother when there was the beautiful harlequin puppet dancing and prancing before her, pirouetting and leaping, bowing and twirling? Mrs Reynolds sighed and left, determined to get on while her daughter was preoccupied.

Emma gave herself up to the puppet show entirely. The music had stopped now and the puppets were talking, but Emma wasn't interested in the story and she wished that the puppet master wouldn't keep putting on those silly voices. It was all so ugly, and yet the children around her seemed so intent on laughter. She didn't find the puppets funny in the least and resented the attempts of the puppet master to garner laughs and coarse guffaws, when all she wanted was to see the beautiful puppets dance and twirl.

Mrs Reynolds did eventually come back and by chance her return coincided with the end of the show. She was relieved to forego the scene that would no doubt have taken place had she insisted that Emma leave before it was finished. She wondered how she had produced such a wilful daughter.

Emma put up no resistance to leaving. She felt a terrible sadness when the curtain fell, and the greyness of the town seemed to seep back into the world around her. But this feeling would only have been intensified had she stayed to see the puppet master pack away the puppets. Emma wanted to remember them as they were in the show.

She trailed behind her mother, who was just explaining that they should hurry across the road to Madame Claudette's Hat and Ribbon Shop – for they both needed new hats for their cousin's wedding – when Emma took one last look back towards the puppet show and walked straight into somebody.

'I'm so sorry,' she said.

She had bumped into a boy of about her own age, but he made no reply. He was staring at her in the most peculiar manner and at first Emma thought she might have stunned him in some way.

There was something about the boy's vacant expression that made Emma shudder. His pale grey, red-rimmed eyes stared out without any hint of life or soul at work behind them. It took Emma a few moments to realise that she knew him.

His name was Gerald, though it was only with considerable difficulty that she could match this sad creature to the boy who had shown her such interest at the church fete. Gerald, like Emma, was quite portly, but he was handsome in spite of this. Somehow this made his present state all the more troubling. He stretched out his arms towards her, opened his mouth and moaned loudly. Emma backed away with a shriek that caused her mother to stop in her tracks and turn round.

'You should pay attention to where you are going, young lady,' said a voice to Emma's right.

Emma turned and saw a formidable-looking woman in a large and rather macabre hat with curving feathers that reminded her of a huge spider.

'You might have knocked poor Gerald over, you silly girl.'

'I'll thank you not to adopt that tone with my daughter,' said Emma's mother, stepping into the fray.

She may have been slight, but Emma's mother was not at all shy in expressing her views, though they were often spoken in a voice that might kindly be described as shrill.

'Your daughter should be more careful,' said Gerald's mother.

'If the boy is going to stand about in the street like a great sack of potatoes, then he is bound to be walked into!' said Mrs Reynolds.

The boy's mother flared her nostrils and, grabbing her son's hand, led him away.

'Well, really!' Emma's mother exclaimed.

'Some people!' said Mrs Timpson-Green, the florist, who had come out of her shop to observe the confrontation. 'But, as a Christian, you have to have some sympathy for the lad.'

'Oh yes,' said Emma's mother, who held Mrs Timpson-Green in very high regard. 'As a Christian.'

She moved closer and tilted her head con-spiratorially.

'Apparently it happened all of a sudden,' she said in a whisper.

'I know,' said Mrs Timpson-Green. 'The doctors are mystified. They say there was a case just like it in Harrogate last month.'

Emma's mother leaned a little closer still and dropped her voice even further, so that Emma could no longer hear. She watched as Gerald and his mother disappeared into the crowd and out of view. But before they did, Gerald turned to stare at her one last time.

Oh, how that gaze unsettled her. To be looked at so intently and yet at the same time so lifelessly, so witlessly – it was as if a shop window mannequin had turned its sculpted, empty head to follow her. She hoped fervently that she might never see that awful face again.

Emma and her mother were in Madame Claudette's for some time, and each passing minute sur-rounded by the comforting loveliness of Emma's favourite shop acted as a much-needed salve to the upset caused by the encounter with Gerald.

After the ribbon shop, they bought some writing paper and then spent an exceedingly dull half-hour in the post office, queuing to send a letter to

Emma's aunt who lived in Canada.

On their way home they walked past the market. The puppet theatre was closed and getting ready to leave. Some of the stallholders were starting to pack up too, shouting out the prices of bargains and behaving in an altogether too forward way, which provoked the sourest of expressions from Emma's mother.

Then, just as they were turning the corner into Pond Street to walk down the hill and back home, Gerald appeared once more, grunting and waving from the kerbside, tugging at his mother's arm.

There was something deeply disturbing about the way he fixed Emma with his dull gaze and waved his arms around, as if he wanted nothing more than to be able to lurch across the road and attack her.

She quickened her pace and tried to avoid his gaze by looking back towards the market, but this seemed to incense him further. He broke free of his mother's grip and came lumbering towards her.

Emma, in her panic, slipped and fell. When she tried to get up, Gerald was already beside her, grabbing her hair with one hand and waving and pointing with the other.

Mrs Reynolds stepped in and slapped Gerald

hard around the side of the face. He didn't cry or even look at Emma's mother. He merely stood staring at Emma in silence for a moment, before suddenly emitting a horrible cry.

'How dare you strike my boy?' said Gerald's mother, rushing over. 'I have a good mind to fetch a policeman.'

'Please do,' said Mrs Reynolds, 'and I shall tell him how your lunatic child tried to murder my daughter.'

Gerald's mother glared at her with a look of bitter resignation, as if she had only just realised with whom she was dealing. Emma sobbed mournfully, begging to be taken home.

'Really!' said Mrs Reynolds. 'I wonder at that creature being allowed out, I really do.'

'How can you be so cruel?' said Gerald's mother. 'He means no harm. Your daughter has upset him in some way. I have never seen him like this before.'

'My daughter has done nothing at all to the boy,' said Emma's mother, raising her long nose to the clouded sky. 'Come along, Emma, before that wild thing breaks free and attacks the both of us.'

The meeting with the horrid, lumpen creature

Gerald had become had upset Emma so much that, try as she might, she could no longer visualise the loveliness of the puppet show, and she had hoped to replay its beauty for weeks to lighten the monotony of her life. That beast had spoiled it for her and, though she knew it was terribly wrong to blame the blameless, still she hated him for it.

Emma was forced to endure her mother reliving the whole episode over supper, when she recounted the incident with added theatrical flourishes for Emma's father, who, as usual, did little to disguise his lack of interest in anything other than the price of cotton.

Emma was sent to bed early with a cup of warm milk, because her mother was certain she must have been horribly traumatised by the shock of being preyed upon by 'that awful creature'.

Ordinarily Emma would have resisted her mother's attentions, but on this occasion she felt that there was a grain of truth in the idea that she had been deeply affected. She was happy to seek the comfort of her bed and the oblivion of sleep.

But Emma's sleep was not a peaceful one: her thoughts were invaded by the unwanted memories of Gerald – of the strange, empty shell of the boy she had once briefly known and, though it pained her to recall it now, liked more than a little.

As in the worst nightmares, there was a ghastly confluence of the real and unreal worlds: she dreamed that she was in the room in which she now slept, except that in her dream she had been woken by a strange sound somewhere in the house.

Far off in the hallway downstairs, she heard the front door swing open and then close. She heard the sound of shuffling footsteps. With the horrible certainty of dreams, Emma knew it was Gerald.

She ran to the landing and leaned over the banister. She saw him standing in the hall, his back to the door, staring up at her with his awful, lifeless, dull grey eyes.

Emma opened her mouth to scream but no sound emerged. She screamed silently until her lungs hurt. Then, with a suddenness made all the more startling by his previous stillness, the boy began to shuffle towards the stairs.

Emma was momentarily frozen, and stared in trembling horror as the boy climbed the staircase with an awkward speed.

It was not until he had reached the top of the stairs and was shuffling towards her down the hall that she finally managed to prise her feet from the floor and run back to her room, slamming the door behind her.

She knew it was a dream. She told herself over and over it was a dream, as the footsteps came closer and closer, closer and closer. Then the door handle gave a terrifying rattle.

Emma woke with a start, still reeling from the nightmare. The real and imagined worlds were so confusingly intermingled that she wondered if she had woken from one dream into another. She could feel beads of sweat on her forehead.

Then she heard the sound of footsteps. They were small and hurried and quiet and so at first they appeared as though they were a long way away. But no. They were in the room. They were in the room; she was certain of it.

Her mind was still escaping the tangle of thoughts that remained from her nightmare, and she struggled to make sense of what she was hearing. Her eyes were gradually adjusting to the gloom of the bedroom. The footsteps had fallen silent.

Suddenly there was a crash that sent Emma scrabbling back on her bed, pulling the covers to her face as she pressed herself up against the wall.

Something unseen had knocked over the vase that stood on her dressing table, and was now behind the curtain. The heavy fabric bulged and twitched as the thing moved about behind it.

Then, all at once, the curtains jerked wildly and shook as whatever it was appeared to climb them; a dark shape scampered across the windowsill and disappeared out through the open window.

Once absolutely sure it had gone, Emma quickly went across to the window and shut it, lest it should try to re-enter. The night was overcast and moonless, but it was midsummer and the sky still bore a dull glow from the day's reluctant departure. By this pale insipid light, she caught a glimpse of something fleeing across the garden. It was a glimpse only, but she had a strange feeling of recognition.

As she went to pull the curtain across, Emma's toe stubbed against something sharp, and she bent down to see that there was a pair of scissors lying on the floor. And not just scissors.

On the floor and on the sill were strands of hair: strands she took at first to be the fur of whatever creature had entered the room, until she realised that the hair was her own. A great hank of hair had been cut from her head.

In a blinding flash she remembered the groaning Gerald, the hand reaching out and grasping her hair, the awful blank intensity of that soulless face.

Emma opened her mouth and screamed, and this

time there was most definitely a sound, and within seconds her father came running into the room, Emma oblivious, her eyes closed tight. She continued to scream and scream until he slapped her with some force across the side of the face.

It was many hours before her parents were able to settle Emma, and she had only fallen asleep through utter exhaustion. The following day it took all of her father's powers of reason and persuasion to explain to her that a boy like Gerald – a boy so painfully slow and clumsy – could never have climbed into her room, even if he had the wit to escape from his own house and walk the half-mile to the Reynolds'.

Besides which, the window to Emma's room was a small casement window. A boy of Gerald's build could never have squeezed through it.

Emma had clearly had a nightmare and gone sleepwalking under its influence. She must somehow have picked up the scissors and cut her own hair. Her parents could only be thankful that she had not injured herself.

Emma took a while to accept the truth of these facts – but in the end she could see no other explanation. Even so, she made sure that the window was thoroughly shut before she went to sleep the following night, and her mother, just to be on the safe side, removed her scissors from the room.

It was some days before Mrs Reynolds felt her daughter had recovered enough to be taken into town. There was always the danger that they might bump into that dreadful boy and his mother, but that was a risk they would have to take. If they stayed away from town for too long, it would look as though they had done something wrong. Mrs Reynolds knew how people gossiped. She knew only too well.

Emma had been dreading this expedition and had feigned a stomach ache to avoid it. But she knew that she couldn't stay in her house for ever. Only the lure of a trip to the ribbon shop and the hope that the puppet show might be back in the market square persuaded her to swallow her fears.

But Madame Claudette's was so crowded that Emma's mother ended up flouncing out, pulling Emma away before she even had time to look at a beautiful pink ribbon that would have been perfect for her new bonnet.

On top of that, the marketplace was full of all kinds of stalls and barrows, but quite devoid of the one thing Emma so longed to see – the puppet theatre.

Then, to make Emma's misery complete, they walked out of the pharmacist's to find Gerald standing on the pavement across the road.

Emma stepped back, bumping into Mr Cartwright, the minister, who paused only to tip his hat and apologise for getting in her way. Emma's mother tried to engage him in conversation, but he seemed to be in a hurry to get on. Meanwhile, Gerald had begun to walk towards Emma.

Mr Reynolds had had a long talk with his daughter about this meeting and what Emma should do if and when it occurred. She was not to confuse the boy of her nightmare with this poor creature who was not responsible for his actions. If she remained calm, Gerald would lose interest in her.

But now, with Gerald standing in front of her, reaching out towards her hair again, Emma found it harder than she had imagined to stay calm. And it had been fairly difficult even in her imagination.

If anything, the dead-eyed face was worse than she had remembered it. There were dark shadows under those awful pale eyes that made the dull whites stand out under the heavy lids. The grey irises that had been so beautiful when there was a light behind them now seemed like those of a blind man.

'What do you want?' whimpered Emma. 'Why are you looking at me? Why are you following me?'

'Emma!' whispered her mother. 'Please control yourself. You haven't been well but you really must show some restraint. You've become obsessed with this creature and it must stop. He is a simpleton. He cannot help it. You must learn to ignore him.'

'That simpleton, as you call him, is my son,' said Gerald's mother coldly, appearing suddenly beside them and looking at Emma with disdain.

'Well, he's upsetting my daughter,' said Mrs Reynolds, immediately on the defensive, roused by the woman's hostile tone.

'My son is doing nothing, madam. He is certainly not being rude or offensive.'

'Perhaps he ought not to be in such crowded places,' said Emma's mother with a purse of her lips.

Gerald made a sudden lurch towards Emma and she could stand it no longer. She turned on her heels and ran, blundering blindly through the crowd, her mother calling after her.

She burst out into an alleyway, cobbled and dark, great warehouses towering overhead on one side, a high wall on the other. The only other sign of life in the alley besides herself was a gaily coloured cart she took a few moments to realise was the puppet show she had enjoyed so much.

'Now, then,' said the puppet master with a smile, appearing around the side of the cart. 'And what have we here?'

Emma had always been told never to talk to strangers, and ordinarily she would have walked away from this odd little man with his waxed moustache and garish make-up, but on this occasion she felt that he was by far the lesser of two evils.

'Please,' said Emma. 'There is a boy. He's following me.'

The puppet master's eyebrows went up and down and he grinned, tapping the side of his nose.

'Aha!' he said. 'The course of true love and so on.'

Emma blushed and frowned.

'No,' she said. 'It's not like that at all.'

'Never mind,' said the puppet master. 'We shall hide you, shan't we, boys and girls?'

It took Emma a couple of seconds to realise he was talking to the puppets in the back of the cart, who were hanging rather forlornly from a frame.

'How do you do, young madam,' said the puppet master with a bow. 'I am very pleased to make your acquaintance.'

'How do you do,' said Emma, casting a worried

glance over her shoulder. 'I saw your show not long ago.'

'You did?' he said. 'And did you enjoy it?'

'Oh yes,' said Emma. 'I love puppets. I love the costumes. I love the dancing. I love everything about them.'

'Really?' said the puppet master, clapping his hands together. 'Well, that's wonderful. That's just wonderful.'

Emma smiled. He seemed genuinely moved.

'Listen,' he said, turning to root about in the cart. 'As you enjoy puppets so much, I may have something of interest.'

He continued his search until he made a small cry and turned round holding a puppet.

'Oh, she's beautiful!' Emma gasped.

'Looks a little like you, doesn't she?' said the puppet master with an arch of one eyebrow.

And it was true: the puppet did look a little like Emma. In fact, it was rather a lot like her, wearing a dress like hers and a neat pair of boots that looked like the ones she had begged her mother for. The hair was especially like hers.

'Is that real hair?' said Emma, but then she noticed that the puppet master was holding another puppet at his side. That one also looked rather familiar.

It was a perfect miniature of Gerald in every way except that, strangely, the puppet version had more life than the living one. Its face seemed animated by comparison.

'Dance for the lady,' said the puppet master.

To Emma's amazement, the puppet that looked like Gerald, and the others hanging from the frame, began to move about slowly.

'Come on,' said the puppet master, an angry note in his voice. 'Do you call that dancing? Dance!'

The puppets responded by speeding up their movements until they were cavorting wildly about.

'How do you do that?' said Emma, smiling at the capering puppets. The puppet master tapped the side of his nose again and winked.

'I cannot tell you all my secrets now, can I?' he said. 'Here. You can have a look at Harlequin if you like.'

And without a reply from Emma, he placed the puppet of the harlequin in her hands. She gasped. It was exquisite. Then it moved. It turned its head and looked at her.

Emma dropped the puppet to the ground as though it were white hot, and the puppet master laughed. It was another clever trick, thought Emma. How on earth had he done it? But even as she had these thoughts, the harlequin puppet got to its tiny feet and walked back to the puppet master. Emma felt suddenly dizzy.

Of course. This is what she had seen, and half recognised, running across the lawn the night of her dream. It was he who had been in her room, he who had cut her hair and taken it and brought it back to this man, so that he could make a puppet of her with her own hair. But why?

Emma suddenly experienced a feeling of falling, a breathless collapsing, as if she were drifting through space like thistledown, drifting on a warm summer wind.

Then, all at once, she was looking back at herself, looking back as she felt the rumble of cartwheels beneath her, looking back at the empty girl in the alleyway who had been Emma but was now barely anything at all, save for blood and bones and pale, tired flesh.

The better part of that which had been Emma swayed gently in the frame. She turned to face the Gerald puppet and realised too late that the boy he had been was trying to warn her, even in her dreams – to frighten her away from the puppet show and the fate that she would share. But to no avail.

'Come along, my beauties,' said the puppet

master. 'Time to find some new children to play with.'

And with that he flicked the reins and the cart gathered speed, clattering away down the cobbled alley.

It was as if my life force had been likewise taken from me, as again I felt myself drifting away, so that though I could hear the Woman in White, her voice sounded increasingly ethereal and echoey.

'Do you enjoy the theatre?' she was saying.

'I used to like puppet shows as a child,' I said, pulling myself together. 'Whenever we saw one I would always rush over to watch. I had to be prised away. I always found them fascinating.'

'Rather like Emma,' she said with a grin.

'Yes, I suppose so,' I answered, not entirely convinced that I wanted to be linked with that unfortunate girl. 'I think I was always a bit frightened by the puppets though,' I added, remembering the odd frisson of trepidation their little painted faces would induce in me.

The image of that cart filled with hanging puppets burst into my mind like a bolt of lightning.

I could almost hear the cart clattering away, and once again I had the distinct impression of something else just out of my sightline, something that was there but that I couldn't make myself see. All I knew was that it was something more terrible than the puppet master.

'And what of real theatre?' said the Woman in White. 'What of real, live actors?'

I was happy to rid myself of the vision and, shaking my head drunkenly, blushed at an amusing recollection. She raised an eyebrow. I grinned sheepishly.

'A few of us from my last school travelled up to London one Saturday and went to the music hall. It was deuced good fun. There was a man who escaped from a tank full of water, and a dog that could sing the National Anthem.'

'It sounds delightful,' she said.

'I'm afraid some of the humour there would shock you,' I said.

She smiled.

'There was one lady who . . .' I began, but I saw no polite way of describing what the lady actually did, and so I looked bashfully towards the sleeping Bishop and rubbed my hands together.

'And what of real theatre?' she asked. 'What of

the Bard, of Shakespeare?'

'I don't think I've seen enough to pass judgement,' I said. 'My father took me to see *Macbeth* once. That was very entertaining.'

'Ah – *Macbeth*,' she said. 'An excellent choice. And why do you think you enjoyed that play so much?'

These words took an age to reach my ears, as if there were a ravine between us rather than a few feet of floor. The air seemed to have congealed and I felt as though we were suspended in aspic. I fixed all my remaining powers of attention on the Woman in White and tried to make my brain form an answer.

'Well,' I said. 'I suppose I like the story of the witches and the premonition and so on, despite what you have said about my love of the rational. And I do like gruesome stories, as you know; *Macbeth* does have a lot of blood and murder and ghosts and what not.'

'Yes it does,' she said.

I closed my eyes for an instant, but immediately opened them after experiencing an awful sensation of falling.

'And of course I like anything to do with history,' I went on. 'Knights and warriors and all that. I'd love to be able to travel back in time and see what it was really like in those days.'

'Would you?' she said with no enthusiasm. Girls never did seem as interested in these things somehow. That was part of the reason they were such poor company, in my opinion.

'Oh yes,' I said. 'Wouldn't it be marvellous to be able to stand and watch the Battle of Hastings or the Siege of Troy? I can't imagine anything more exciting.'

The Woman in White gave me a rather pitying look.

'Battlefields are less exciting than you might think.'

She said these words with a strange and cold authority for one who couldn't possibly have had any experience of warfare. But then it hit me.

'Are you perhaps a nurse, miss?' I said, wagging an index finger in the air in the manner of a university professor solving a particularly taxing mathematical problem.

She cocked her head and smiled.

'No,' she said after a moment. 'No, dear boy, I am not a nurse. Though I have often been called upon to visit the sick, and the sick have, I hope, sometimes taken comfort in those visits.'

The Woman in White looked down at her watch.

'What is the time?' I asked.

'But I have another story for you,' she said. 'Would you like to hear it?'

I frowned at her lack of response to my question but I couldn't hold her gaze and, with a sigh, nodded my agreement. To be honest, I felt too weary to argue.

'Lovely,' she said, tapping her fingertips together. 'It concerns a nun.'

'Really?' I said.

'Yes,' she said jauntily. 'Her name was . . . Well, you shall see what her name was. Let's begin.'

8

SISTER VERONICA

Sister Veronica ran the back of her hand across her forehead, mopping up the beads of perspiration that had gathered there. She breathed deeply through her nose, her nostrils flaring as she did so. She composed herself and smiled her brilliant white smile, a smile that Mother Superior had said could light up the darkest of hours.

'You can shout and scream as much as you like, silly child,' she said. 'These old walls are awful thick and we are a long way from town. No one is going to hear you and no one would care if they could.'

Sister Veronica lifted the hazel switch above her

right shoulder and brought it down, its angular trajectory marked by a high-pitched whistle until it hit the bare legs of the girl with a brittle crack.

The girl squealed in pain and Sister Veronica pursed her lips before raising the switch and bringing it down again. Whistle. Crack. Squeal.

Sister Veronica closed her eyes and let her heartbeat slow its giddy fluttering. The girl whimpered and sobbed, pressing her face into her outstretched arms, the knuckles standing out as she clutched the edge of the tabletop. Slowly, Sister Veronica came out of her trance.

'Come, child,' she said, the usual headache forming. 'We must all endeavour to be more like the saints, who bore their sufferings with such grace and fortitude and dignity.'

The girl winced and slid from the table, walking as best as she could to stand with the watching girls.

'Though, of course,' continued Sister Veronica, 'the blessed saints would not have been caught stealing from the kitchens now, would they?'

Sister Veronica allowed herself a smile at this joke, but it faded fast as smiles will when they are starved of company. The girls had heard Sister Veronica's thoughts on the dignified suffering of

the saints many times before – many, many times.
These words were often accompanied by her wide
and white-toothed smile. And a beating.

'Now then, girls,' said Sister Veronica, though she
was scarcely more than a girl herself. It had not
been so many years since she was among their
number. 'As you all knew of Christine's sin of theft
and did not report it, none of you will be attending
the village fete this year.'

Like a showman working a crowd in a music
hall, Sister Veronica left a pause for the groan she
was sure would come, but there was silence.

'Instead,' she continued, 'we will see if we cannot
improve those shabby souls of yours. We will use
this time in the study of art, which God has gifted
to man alone among his creations, so that we might
be given some small glimmer of knowledge of the
glory that is heaven.'

Again, Sister Veronica was surprised that no
grumble or moan greeted this speech. In fact, the
girls seemed to be listening in rapt attention.
Perhaps she was finally getting through to these
poor creatures.

For though Sister Veronica, in the dark minutes
before sleep pulled her under, was plagued by
doubts – terrible, terrible doubts – she truly

believed that it was her calling to bring these girls to a state of grace.

Sister Veronica felt that it was part of this calling to bestow some of her appreciation of art upon her girls – though only of religious art, of course, not the vulgar French paintings with which her father had filled the family house.

A true work of art, for Sister Veronica, was one that brought her closer to God, that transported her out of the grubby, dull concerns of the mortal world.

But these girls were so dull and their concerns were so very mortal. There was only one among them who showed the slightest feeling for the divine ecstasy that a painting might evoke; only Barbara seemed to truly appreciate the wonderful otherness of art. But now, even Barbara was lost to her.

Barbara blamed her for what happened to Mary McGreevy, she knew that. But how could she be held responsible for the fate of that ridiculous girl? How could she possibly be blamed for the fact that silly Mary McGreevy was constantly in trouble?

Sister Veronica had been charged with disciplining the girl, and had she not been a nasty, ill-tempered and vindictive little minx, she would not have needed to be punished so often.

Sister Veronica herself had been beaten back when she was just plain Catherine Connor, had she not? She had been foolish and frivolous and tempted by sin and she had been beaten. It had made her strong. It had given her a brief and sacred insight into the sufferings of the saints. It had brought her to God.

But Mary McGreevy was never going to see the light of His grace. She could never understand what it meant to serve anyone but herself. And if further proof was needed of the girl's hell-bound nature, she finally committed the dreadful sin of suicide.

Barbara, sweet Barbara, had insisted – inexplicably, infuriatingly – on regarding silly, wilful Mary McGreevy as a special friend. Sister Veronica had seen them talking and giggling like village girls and had been surprised at how angry it had made her. All the girls had seemed in thrall to Mary. But how could a girl like Barbara keep company with such a flighty thing? It was unaccountably vexing.

And now, ever since that foolish child had consigned herself to hell by taking her own life, Barbara had barely spoken to Sister Veronica. She had taken to staring at her during mass in a quite insolent way. Had it been any of the other girls, Sister Veronica would have beaten them; oh, how she would have beaten them. But she could not do that to Barbara. Not Barbara.

'Do you see here, children?' said Sister Veronica with a smile so bright it made the nearest girl flinch, pointing to one of the small paintings showing the Stations of the Cross. 'This is St Veronica, after whom I am named.' She smiled, letting that fact sink in, biting the inside of her cheek with the dark thrill of being so near to the sin of pride. 'See how she wipes the blessed brow of our dear Lord?'

Sister Veronica stared at the picture with a faraway expression on her face: an expression that the girls had to come to both recognise and fear.

'Can any of you, I wonder, imagine what that must have been like, to have been so close to our Saviour and to have been of service to Him in His hour of struggle?'

None of the girls answered. They had learned by long and painful experience that anything they said might bring on one of Sister Veronica's rages. Silence could also bring on a rage, of course, but on the whole it seemed safer to simply return her gaze without any comment or expression. Sister Veronica looked at the girls through half-closed eyes and shook her head.

'But how could you?' she said. 'How could girls such as you understand a thing like that? How could you understand what it is to put yourself at the service of others, as St Veronica did and as we do here?'

Sister Veronica took her art classes very seriously. She was not without some talent herself, though she tried not to take too much pride in the fact; sometimes she had to punish herself by destroying a drawing she was especially fond of, and she hated to do that.

Some girls from the school had gone on to be governesses in some of the finest houses in England and the Colonies. Sister Ruth had told her only the other day of receiving a letter from a girl she had taught who was now a governess in a house in the Bahamas.

Sister Veronica had been tempted by a pang of jealousy when Sister Ruth, who was far too excitable for Sister Veronica's liking, had told her about the letter. She had never received a letter from a girl who had been in her care. Such was the ingratitude of girls like these. Besides, Sister Ruth had recounted a tale from the letter that was most inappropriate in its reference to 'handsome young

185

men' and Sister Veronica had been forced to say that she had something urgent to attend to in order to bring the conversation to a close.

'Now, girls,' said Sister Veronica, loudly enough to make tiny Susan Tiller jump. 'We are to do some drawing. I can think of no better way for you to spend the time you would otherwise have wasted on the Godless nonsense at the village fete or ogling the village boys – yes, I mean you, Margaret.'

Margaret made no response. Just the mention of boys usually elicited giggles, but not today. Sister Veronica frowned.

'I thought that we might return to the still life that we –'

'Sister Veronica.'

Sister Veronica spun like a snake in the direction of the interruption – how she hated to be interrupted – but saw that it was Barbara who had her hand raised, and was that a smile on her face?

'Yes, Barbara,' she said. 'What is it?'

'Beg your pardon, Sister Veronica,' she said, stepping forward, 'but we've been talking, haven't we, girls?'

The girls all nodded excitedly and said yes.

'We were wondering, Sister Veronica, if we might do a drawing of you.'

Sister Veronica willed herself, a little unsuccessfully, not to blush, and she dug her fingernails into her palms, angry at how flustered and girlish she felt.

'Me, child?' she said, smiling brightly. 'Why, I don't know . . .'

'You're worried about the sin of vanity, aren't you, Sister Veronica?' said Barbara.

Sister Veronica's smile disappeared. She did worry about the sin of vanity. She had worried about this often. She knew she was pretty, but she tried very hard not to take pride in it.

'We knew you would be,' said Barbara. 'I said to Margaret, "Sister Veronica will not let us do a drawing of her. She would never want to put herself forward in that way. She would think it blasphemous."'

'I'm not sure it would be blasphemous exactly,' said Sister Veronica. The light suddenly faded in the room as a cloud passed in front of the sun and the gloom made her smile seem all the brighter. 'But vanity *is* a terrible sin. Do you know why?'

'Because it distracts us from our love of the Lord, Sister,' said Barbara.

'Well done, Barbara,' she said, beaming. 'And so we must always be on our guard. So shall we return to the still life?'

'We knew you would not want us to draw a picture of you as yourself,' said Barbara.

'I'm not following you, child,' said Sister Veronica, moving towards the still-life table.

'That's why we came up with the idea,' said Barbara. 'Oh please, please say you will, Sister Veronica. Please.'

Sister Veronica turned to her patiently.

'But I do not know what you mean, Barbara,' she said.

'Oh – sorry, Sister,' said Barbara with a giggle. 'We thought that you might pose as a saint for us.'

Sister Veronica felt slightly light-headed. Not only was Barbara talking to her again, but the girls wanted her to pose as one of the blessed saints. It was like a dream. Not that she would ever have allowed herself to dream such a thing.

'And what saint would that be now?'

'We thought we would ask you to pose and then we would see if you could guess.'

Sister Veronica looked at the gaggle of excited, expectant faces in front of her. Were they making fun of her? She found it hard to let her guard down, but she did not want to break the spell of that moment.

Mother Superior had once chided her for not

having a sense of humour. 'Sometimes it pays to show you are a good sport,' she had said. Could she be a 'good sport' now? She wasn't sure. For Barbara's sake, maybe she could.

'Very well, then,' said Sister Veronica, smiling patiently. 'How shall I stand?'

'We would like you to stand against a column,' said Barbara. 'You know – as if you were tied to it.'

Sister Veronica walked over to one of the columns that stood in the classroom. The builders of the convent had placed a row of them at one side of the room, making the place impractical in so many ways, but giving it the aura of a chapel – something Sister Veronica had always loved. A sudden flash of sunlight splashed coloured light from the stained-glass windows across the stonework: gold, green and blood red.

Sister Veronica leaned against the column, but Barbara instructed her to stretch her arms back as if she had her hands tied behind it. She did as Barbara asked, wondering to herself for how long she would be able to hold such an uncomfortable position, however much of a good sport she intended to be.

'Can you guess which saint it is yet, Sister Veronica?' asked Barbara.

'Am I perhaps to be St Sebastian?' she asked, a slight tremor in her voice at the thought. There was an engraving of St Sebastian in the book of saints that was a particular favourite of hers, though she often worried that her enjoyment of it was not seemly.

'No, Sister Veronica,' said Barbara. 'Not St Sebastian.'

Sister Veronica frowned, going through the book of saints in her mind, trying to recall if any of the other saints were tied to a column, but she could only think of Jesus himself, tied to a column to be flogged before his crucifixion, and she could not allow herself to dwell on such a blasphemous idea.

She realised, as she listed the saints in her mind, that she saw them only in terms of their martyrdoms and not their works. This was how they were so often depicted in the paintings and prints that Sister Veronica loved to look at.

She always pictured St Bartholomew holding his own skin over one shoulder like a cloak, as a reminder of his blessed martyrdom: he was flayed alive. So it was with St James the Less and the club that was used to beat him to death, St Paul with the sword that beheaded him, St Blaise and the iron combs used to tear his flesh and St Laurence with the griddle on which he was roasted. Lost among these thoughts, Sister Veronica suddenly became aware of hands grabbing hers and something being wrapped around her wrists.

'Girls,' she said, trying to wriggle free from the rope. No – not rope, she realised: wire. 'That is rather painful, I'm afraid.'

Margaret stepped out from behind the column, grinning.

'Do you hear me, Margaret?' she snarled. 'Release me this instant.'

'Can you still not guess, Sister?' said Margaret in response.

'Now you're making me cross, girls,' said Sister Veronica.

'Come along now, Sister,' said one of the other girls. 'Guess.'

'I do not want to guess!' roared Sister Veronica. 'I want you to release me this instant!'

The girls giggled.

'Maybe these will give you a clue,' said Barbara, producing a large pair of pliers she had found in the stables. Sister Veronica had seen the grounds-man use them to tug a huge rusting nail from a fence post.

She pulled once again at the wire that held her

wrists but the movement only seemed to tighten the binds, and they cut into her flesh and made her wince.

'Come now, Sister Veronica,' said Barbara, turning to the other girls with a grin. 'Surely you can guess.'

But Sister Veronica had already guessed.

'This has gone far enough!' said Sister Veronica in a voice she had intended to sound authoritative but which instead came out thin and pleading.

'You can scream as much as you like, silly child,' said Barbara in a voice Sister Veronica realised must be an imitation of her own. 'But no one will hear you.'

Barbara nodded at the girls and Sister Veronica felt hands grabbing at her face, one holding her jaw and another attaching something to her nose. It was a clothes peg. Barbara stepped forward with a look of grim intent.

'Oh dear Lord!' gasped Sister Veronica. 'Oh God!'

St Apollonia. There was a rather unpleasant engraving of her in *The Lives of the Saints*: a podgy-faced woman holding a pair of pincers a bit like those Barbara was opening and closing in front of her. St Apollonia: whose martyrdom had involved having all her teeth pulled out while bound to a column. St Apollonia: patron saint of dentists.

The clothes peg pinched her nostrils painfully and the blurred shape of it all but blocked out Barbara and the approaching pliers.

The image of those pliers lingered unpleasantly and there was, I felt, something about the Woman in White that made it easy to imagine her holding them. But despite this unsettling thought I yawned deeply and struggled to stay alert. The cumulative effect of these tales, however alarming they were, was that of a series of bedtime stories, for I was becoming drowsier and drowsier.

I should say, though, that it was a test of my memory to recall being told a bedtime story – my parents had never set much store by such things – and the effort unexpectedly brought forward an image of the very governess I had mentioned earlier and whom I had so cruelly used.

Remembering the image of her smiling face as she wished me goodnight and the soft *clump* of the closing book pricked me with guilt and shame. The Woman in White seemed to detect this emotion in my face and gave me a curious look.

...th I was finding it increasingly difficult to ...ain eye contact with her. I had an awful ...ing that it was only a matter of time before I would be joining the other members of the carriage in deep slumber.

In an attempt to disguise this soporific state to the Woman in White, who seemed as bright and alert as ever, I adopted a rather contrived, chirpy tone and slapped my hands together loudly.

'Well, well,' I said. 'Are we still not moving, then? Perhaps I should get out and wander up to see the driver.'

I made to stand, but without even putting weight on my legs I knew it would be futile. I simply did not have the strength to get up. I felt sure that had I tried to stand, I should have made the most frightful fool of myself by falling to the floor. I was relieved when the Woman in White put out a restraining hand.

'No, no,' she said, holding my arm. 'That would never do. You must not leave the train when it is at the tunnel's mouth.'

'Really?' I said. 'But –'

'Really,' she said, as if the matter were now closed for discussion. 'It is quite out of the question.'

'Oh,' I said, settling back into my chair and trying

to focus; the Woman in White had become strangely blurred. 'I had no idea there was such a rule.'

'Yes,' she said. 'It is an absolute rule, I assure you.'

Even in my foggy-minded state, I found it hard to believe that this woman had any special insight into the workings of the railway company, but until I felt more able to act on my statements, I had little choice but to quietly accept it as true.

I cast a weary glance at the other passengers, whose sleep carried on unabated and whose oblivion now seemed attractive, where once it had been irritating. But the thought of sleeping while the Woman in White remained awake somehow filled me with a deep unease, though I could never have said why.

'What time is it, please?' I asked her, having looked out of the window and seen that the light was fading fast. The sky had a sickly pallor to it and the bank was almost all beshadowed.

'You sound so tired,' she said soothingly. 'Please don't feel the need to stay awake for politeness' sake. I am quite at home in my own company. Please. Close your eyes if you wish.'

Oh, how I longed to do just that, but her requesting it of me merely increased my certainty that I should do nothing of the sort.

She seemed to sense this resistance and smiled at me, rather as a mother might smile at a wilful child who is avoiding doing something that is really for his own benefit. Still I fought to keep my heavy lids from closing and my mind from giving up to the fog that sought to obfuscate my every thought.

'So,' said the Woman in White after a few moments. 'You are to return to school. Are you the kind of boy who looks forward to the holidays with bated breath?'

'No,' I said. 'If I had my way I would remain at school while my father is away. As I've already said, my stepmother and I do not see eye to eye.'

'And yet she loves you,' she said.

I thought this a very curious supposition and snorted loudly.

'Do you not think it possible for a person to love someone who does not love them?' she asked.

'I don't know,' I said, the pain in my temples from earlier returning for a moment. 'I hadn't thought about it. It has certainly never occurred to me that my stepmother has any special feelings for me.'

The Woman in White smiled.

'Because you do not have any special feeling for her?'

'Yes,' I said. 'No – I don't know. I don't think I want to talk about my stepmother any more.'

'Of course,' she said. 'Of course. We only got on to that subject by my asking you about the school holidays. If you don't enjoy your stepmother's company, they must be an awful bore for you.'

'I spend most of the holidays in the house or in the garden, reading,' I explained.

'Ah yes,' she said. 'Stories can be a great comfort.'

'I'm not sure I seek comfort in books,' I said. 'I don't think I need any comfort. I read to amuse myself, that's all.'

'Well then, perhaps you will allow me to amuse you with another of my stories.'

My headache was now excruciating and so I happily agreed. Trying to hold a conversation was far too taxing.

'As chance would have it,' she said, as I tried to concentrate on her voice and stay awake, 'this story concerns a boy, much like yourself, who found the holidays a bore. But he found a rather different way to pass the time . . .'

9

THE WHISPERING BOY

Roland sucked the air between his teeth with a whistle, winced and shook his head. It was Cutter all right and he was dead for sure. Roland had seen dead bodies before: he had kissed his grandmother's cold grey forehead only a year ago.

But then he had scarcely known his grandmother and her body had lain peacefully at rest in a darkened bedroom, not like this – sprawled in the street like a dog. And he had known Cutter well, liked him even. But he had to appear calm. Leaders were expected to take everything in their stride.

'It's the Whispering Boy!' hissed one of the boys,

pointing with a trembling finger towards the body. 'It's him again, ain't it?'

'Shut up!' said Roland, taking strength from the other boy's fear. It was a game, a kind of race. He did not have to be fearless. He simply had to show less fear than they did. He simply had to be better than they were, and Roland felt more than able to fulfil that requirement.

Since he had returned home for the school holidays, Roland had heard nothing but talk of the Whispering Boy. These idiots seemed to have gathered together to nurture a complete obsession about some nonsensical apparition. That was why they needed Roland. These fools were like witless animals.

'Rabbit's right,' said Jack, his voice small and brittle. 'It's the Whispering Boy for sure.'

Roland sighed and shook his head. He looked at Jack the way a schoolteacher might look at a child who had once again failed to grasp the basic rudiments of Latin grammar.

'You don't know everything, Roland,' said Jack. 'Just because you go to that fancy school of yours.'

'I know I don't believe in any Whispering Boy.'

'Is that right?' said Jack, pointing to Cutter's body. 'Have you seen his face?'

Roland had indeed seen that face, and however

much he blustered for effect – to show he was in control of their little gang – Roland had to admit that Cutter's face was strange. His eyes were wide and so wild that they looked fit to burst from their sockets, the whites of his eyes bloodshot. Roland's forced bravado faltered every time he looked down at that face.

However, though Cutter's eyes were those of someone who had died in terror, screaming their lungs out, his mouth was not. Instead of being stretched open, Cutter's mouth was almost closed, his lips tight and pinched. The contrast between the crazed eyes and the tight mouth would have been comical in a living face. But Roland had already given this some thought.

'I think he was suffocated,' he said, raising his hand to his face in emphasis. 'I think someone clamped their hand over his mouth until he was dead.'

The group murmured and Roland had to resist the temptation to smile. Clearly none of them had considered this.

Roland's father was appalled that his son spent time with these children, but Roland revelled in the chance to lead them. Their ignorance and lack of wit was just what he found so appealing. At school he was never given the opportunity to lord it over anyone. Despite a deep conviction that he was the equal, if not the better, of his peers, they had chosen to ignore his gifts.

But here among the shiftless urchins of his home town, he had found his niche. He was intelligent enough to appear like a sage to these local oafs, and tough and ruthless enough to reinforce his leadership physically if necessary. He thought of himself as a general in charge of a rabble.

'He must have been strong, whoever he was,' said Figg. 'Cutter was strong himself and he wasn't one to give up without a fight. But see – he ain't got a mark on him.'

Figg was right and Roland knew it. Cutter behaved like an animal when riled and whoever did this was someone to be feared, no doubt about that. But it wasn't any boy, whispering or otherwise. This was the work of a man: a big, strong, evil man.

Fighting his revulsion at touching the corpse, Roland leaned down to close Cutter's eyes. He thought it would be a nice touch and he had seen a man do it once when an old fellow had dropped dead outside the Dog and Duck.

But just as he was about to close the eyelids, Roland jerked back, embarrassed to hear the squeal of panic he emitted. Something was moving inside Cutter's mouth.

A fat fly poked its head out into the daylight; its bottle-green body emerged seconds later. The boys all stared, frozen, as the fly gave its wings a tremulous flutter and then took off, buzzing lazily away.

The sound of Norris vomiting behind him brought Roland to his senses.

'I hate flies,' he said.

'Who doesn't!' hissed Jack.

'That's disgusting,' said Rabbit, his voice breaking under the strain of fighting the urge to sob. 'Cover him up, somebody, before every fly in this filthy place crawls down his throat.'

'Cover him?' said Roland. 'What with, precisely? Are you offering your coat?'

'No!' said Rabbit, screwing up his face. 'There's got to be something.' But a quick look round showed that there was not.

'We'd better go and fetch someone instead of just standing here. Otherwise it will look like we did it,' said Jack. 'Norris – go and fetch my pa and tell him what's happened.'

Roland was annoyed that it had been Jack rather than him who had taken the lead, but it was so clearly the right thing to do he could say nothing and merely nodded sullenly as Norris looked to him for confirmation.

Norris was happy to leave Cutter's body and, without saying a word, set off down the hill towards the town centre and the butcher's shop owned by Jack's father.

Roland was calm now. All dread of Cutter's body was gone. Despite Jack's intervention, he felt in control of himself and of the boys around him.

'It's their fault,' said Rabbit, pointing to the navvies working on the new houses. 'It's them what disturbed the graves.'

'Yeah,' said Jack. 'Look at them. What do we need all these houses for? Who wants to see all that brick and slate and sash windows and all that? This ain't London.'

Jack stared at Roland. It was Roland's father who had bought the land and was paying for those houses. Roland grinned and shook his head. Did Jack really think he could intimidate him?

'Who cares what they're building or what they're building it with?' said Rabbit. 'It's the fact that they dug into them graves. It's a plague pit, they say.'

'It ain't a plague pit,' said Figg.

'What is it, then?' said Roland dismissively.

'It's the old workhouse they knocked down

before they started building,' replied Figg. 'There was an outbreak of fever there, a hundred years or so back. There was little children in there and they just locked 'em up and let 'em die. That's what my old man says, anyway.'

'And your father would know, wouldn't he?' said Roland with a sneer. 'He hasn't set foot out of the house for years, except to go down the pub. And it's not as if he's a great one for reading, either.'

'You don't have to read books to know there was a workhouse there,' said Jack coldly. 'Everyone knows that. That's why the Whispering Boy is doing this.'

'There is no Whispering Boy,' said Roland.

'Yes there is.'

'No there isn't,' said Roland.

'*Yes there is*,' said Jack, clenching his fists. 'I seen him with my own eyes.'

Everyone turned to look at him.

'Well, how is it that you haven't mentioned it before?' said Roland.

Jack shook his head.

'I don't know. I suppose I thought you wouldn't believe me,' he said.

'Who says we will now?' said Roland with a smirk.

'Let him talk,' said Figg. 'Go on, Jack. Tell us what you saw.'

'It was the day they found the bricklayer,' said Jack, sitting down on the wall. 'He was the first one, remember. With Cutter, that makes five now.'

'All right,' said Roland. 'We can count.' He smiled at Rabbit. 'Well, most of us can. What about the bricklayer?'

'I saw him just before he died,' said Jack. 'He walked past me, like, and then after a minute or two I heard this weird noise.'

'Whispering?' asked Roland.

'No – not whispering. More like gasping. Or hissing. And then I turned and instead of the bricklayer – who I know now was lying in the ditch with that expression on his face, same as what Cutter has – there was this boy standing there . . . only – I can't rightly explain.'

'Can't explain?' said Roland. 'What did he look like, then?'

'I can't hardly say,' said Jack shaking his head.

'Can't hardly say?' repeated Roland with a grin.

Jack frowned. 'You calling me a liar?'

'I'm not calling you anything,' said Roland. Jack may have been small, but he was tough. He wasn't someone to push too hard unless you were looking for a fight. There would be a time and a place for that, thought Roland. But now wasn't it. 'All I'm saying is either you saw him or you didn't.'

'And I did,' said Jack.

'Well then,' said Roland. 'What did he look like?'

'It ain't that simple,' said Jack. 'One minute there was no one there and the next there was. Then there wasn't again.'

Roland spat and sniffed and turned to Jack with the look of someone who had heard just about everything.

'So when he *was* there – in between the times when he wasn't – *what did he look like?*'

'That's just it,' said Jack. 'He didn't really look like anything.'

'He must have looked like a boy, though,' said Roland, smiling. 'Or else we would be talking about the Whispering Dog or the Whispering Kettle or whatever, wouldn't we?'

'He looked like a boy all right,' said Jack. 'But only the shape of a boy. He was like a shadow or something. It was like he was made out of smoke.'

'Made out of smoke?' said Roland with a laugh. 'Listen to yourself, friend. Made out of smoke?'

'I'm just telling you what I saw,' said Jack. 'Don't ask if you don't want to hear the answer, all right?'

Jack looked at Roland with an expression that left no one in any doubt that as far as he was concerned, the conversation was ended.

Roland promised himself to have that fight with Jack, and to have it soon. He would make sure that when it happened, it would be on his terms. He had already begun to carry a short metal bar in his coat pocket for just such an occasion.

Jack Landon's father, the butcher, arrived in due course, led by Norris. He hailed his son and Jack showed him the body. He had already sent word for the constable and he knelt down and looked at Cutter lying on the patch of wasteland.

Landon had never been fond of the boy, but even so it was a sorry end and his mother would be distraught. He had wanted to see for himself that this was not some kind of evil prank before asking his wife to break the news, but now he sent Norris back down the hill to the shop.

Landon looked at Roland and nodded, acknowledging by force of habit that this boy was the child of gentry. But he did so reluctantly. Roland's father might be rich and a justice of the peace, but Landon didn't like the way he and his family lorded it over everyone. A fly landed on the back of his hand and he flicked it away in disgust. He might need the father, but there was no harm in causing a bit of trouble for the son, he thought to himself. No harm at all.

At dinner that evening, Roland saw his father signal to his mother with a slight tilt of the head, and she got to her feet immediately, saying that she would leave the men to their talking; she had a letter she needed to write. She gave Roland a pained smile as she left.

'Now then,' said Roland's father, lifting his napkin from his lap and dropping it on to the table. 'I thought we might have a little chat, you and I – man to man, as it were.'

He lit a cigar and blew a cloud of noxious grey smoke across the room.

'What would you like to talk about, Father?' said Roland indifferently.

'I bumped into Mr Landon in the bank this afternoon,' he said. 'He tells me that you were there when that poor lad's body was found.'

'Yes, Father,' said Roland. 'I was.'

'Could you tell me what you were doing there?'

'I wasn't doing anything, Father,' he replied. 'I

was with some friends, that's all.'

'Friends,' snorted his father. 'Can you really call that band of pickpockets, and goodness knows what else, your friends?'

'I don't know what you want me to say,' said Roland, looking away.

'Landon tells me you're in league with these ruffians, that you think yourself their leader.'

'His own son is among them!' said Roland, waving his arms in exasperation. 'How can he criticise me?'

'His opinion matters not one jot,' said Roland's father. 'It is I who find this behaviour unacceptable!'

Roland knew that there was no point in replying and so he looked down at his empty plate. A fly was crawling across it and it brought back the memory of Cutter. He made a swipe for it, but missed.

'This has to stop!' said his father.

'Really, Father,' said Roland. 'I can't see what harm it does anyone. Am I not to be allowed to choose my own company?'

'No,' said his father, stubbing out his cigar angrily. 'No, you are not!'

He glared at Roland, and then took a deep

breath, trying to keep his promise to his wife to hold his temper.

'I've spoken to the headmaster at Hethering Court,' he continued after a moment, his voice at a more normal level. 'We have decided that it would be in everyone's interest if you did not return to the school at the end of the holidays.'

This statement took Roland completely by surprise. He had expected some ban on leaving the house or from associating with riff-raff, but not this. He could not stop himself grinning.

'I can see by your expression,' said his father, 'that the idea of ending your time at Hethering Court School will not unduly disturb you.'

'I should say not,' said Roland. 'I can't abide the place.' But then a thought occurred to him. 'Which school am I to go to instead?'

His father laced his fingers together and cracked his knuckles loudly.

'Ah,' he said. 'Well, that's just it. You're not going back to school at all.'

Roland frowned, confused. What exactly was going on here?

'I don't understand,' he said.

'I think we both know that you're never going to amount to very much academically,' said his father.

'Oh, you're clever enough – too clever, I often think – but you don't care about all that, do you?'

Roland didn't reply.

'I was never a great one for books myself, son. Perhaps we have more in common than we think, eh?'

Roland's expression made it transparent that he believed this to be very, very unlikely.

'I have managed to secure you a place in the East India Company,' continued his father. 'You've always wanted to travel.'

'No I haven't,' said Roland.

'You leave for Bombay a week on Tuesday.'

For once Roland was speechless. He stared at his father in disbelief.

'It'll make a man of you, my boy,' he said. 'It'll make a man of you.'

Roland knew that there was nothing to be done. He and his father were not so very different: once he had made up his mind, there would be no changing it. But Roland was determined not to give his father the satisfaction of thinking he had in any way bested him.

Instead Roland accepted his fate without further argument or emotion. Within an hour, he had fully adjusted himself to this new prospect and even saw that it might be an improvement on his tedious life in England.

But he felt that there needed to be some definite break with his past life. It wouldn't feel right to simply step from one life to the next without some kind of marker.

Beside, he had unfinished business. Though it was almost inevitable that Jack Landon would take his place, Roland didn't see why the boy should inherit his leadership so quietly and painlessly. He had no wish to say goodbye to the other members of his gang. He had no affection for any of those boys. The business he had with Jack was for him and him alone.

Roland waited near Landon's butcher's shop on the high street until he saw Jack leaving and heading off through the alleyway that ran alongside. He caught up with him before he had reached the end.

'What do you want?' said Jack, turning at the sound of Roland's voice.

'I just came to tell you I'm going away in a few days,' said Roland.

'Yeah?' said Jack, with a feigned lack of interest. 'Good.'

He began to walk away.

'Meet me up by the new houses,' Roland called after him. 'Where we found Cutter. At sundown. Or are you the coward I always thought you were?'

Jack turned back to face him again.

'I ain't scared of you,' he said calmly. 'I ain't never been scared of you. It's my pa that's scared of your father, that's all. If it wasn't for him I'd have done for you years ago. Sundown it is. I look forward to it.'

Roland had hoped to spook Jack by arranging to meet him at the place they'd found Cutter's body, but it seemed to have had little effect. He had noted the expression on Jack's face: it was one that contemplated victory.

Roland had to admit that Jack would be a formi-dable opponent. He was tough and dogged, proud and strong. But he had one major weakness. Despite his rough and ragged background, he was essentially good and fair-minded.

Roland was ready to exploit this. As he walked back down to the high street, he felt the metal bar in his pocket and smiled. He had no intention of risking defeat at the hands of this ragamuffin. Roland was going to show him why he had been the leader and not Jack.

Perhaps he would put a brick through Landon's

window before he left, too, and teach that fat butcher to keep his nose out of other people's business.

As Roland reached the top of the hill that evening, he could see Jack standing in the shadow of one of the few remaining walls of the old workhouse buildings. He chuckled to himself. Maybe he had Jack all wrong. He had taken him for the kind who would step straight up to a fight, not skulk about in the shadows.

But when Roland walked a little further on, he realised that the figure ahead could not be Jack, for Jack was lying on the road in front of him, flies crawling across his face – a face distorted into the same expression Cutter had worn when they'd found him.

The flies rose as one as Roland cautiously approached and flew towards the boy who stood by the wall. Roland heard the noise, registering the strange hissing, rustling sound that had given the Whispering Boy his name, as the figure began to move out of the darkness.

He took the metal bar from his coat pocket and waved it above his head, taking comfort from the weight of it in his hand. Whoever this boy was, Roland was not going to run. He had never run in his life.

'You think I'm scared of you?' he said, his voice thin and shaking. 'I'll cave your skull in, whoever you are.'

He almost added, 'Whatever you are,' because now that he looked again he could see exactly what Jack had meant by him looking like smoke. He was more shadow than boy. What was he wearing?

The Whispering Boy stopped when Roland spoke. Maybe he had frightened him with the metal. He waved it again. The Whispering Boy began to come towards him.

But this movement was as strange as the boy's appearance, for though the ground on which they both stood was uneven and strewn with brick rubble, the Whispering Boy seemed to move as though he were sliding across a polished ballroom floor. The whispering noise grew in volume.

Roland was beginning to think that running might indeed be the best option and, besides, there was no one here to witness his retreat. But just as he was thinking this, a big fat fly flew straight at him. He nearly brained himself with the metal bar trying to swat it away.

But then another came, and another, and another, and in a few fateful, hideous seconds Roland realised what was happening, though his mind struggled to cope with the information.

The Whispering Boy was only the shape of a boy and nothing more and that shape was formed from flies, countless flies, their sibilant movements causing a continual hiss like the whisper of a thousand souls.

Roland turned to run, but the flies were quicker than even his thoughts. They flew to his face, smothering him, wrapping themselves around his mouth and nose like a living scarf.

Roland clenched his mouth shut and tried to keep the flies out of his nose but he couldn't block it and breathe. His mind struggled against the inevitability of his fate. His lips parted ever so slightly, and the flies took their chance.

The flies re-formed into the shape of the Whispering Boy, though more raggedly this time, as if their discipline was all spent.

Away they went, now in the form of a boy, now merely a cloud of flies, now nothing, now a boy once more. They shimmered and shifted and dissolved until once again they were nothing. Flies and nothing more.

While the Woman in White had been recounting her tale, I had been utterly caught up in it, my mind entirely concentrated on the listening and picturing of the words. I was there. I saw the Whispering Boy. I saw those flies. I witnessed that awful death.

But yet again, I felt that I was not the only witness to those events. Something flickered at the very edge of my vision, something that was never there when I looked, something that was always a blur, a faint trace, a ghostly mirage.

As soon as the story ended, it was as if the listening had used up an enormous amount of my strength and energy. Vampire-like, those tales were draining me.

'What time is it, miss?' I asked again, no longer sure whether she had ever answered.

'It's getting late,' she said, making no attempt to look at her watch.

I was shocked to see that the view outside was now almost monochrome: a vague sketch in shades of blue, while only the very uppermost edge of the bank was lit by the dying sun.

'My grandfather will be so worried,' I said forlornly. 'He will be wondering what has become of me. I wish I could tell him that I was safe.'

'Your grandfather?' said the Woman in White.

218

'Yes,' I said. 'He is meeting me at King's Cross Station and we are going to travel across London together to Charing Cross, where we shall board another train. At least I hope we shall. With all this delay, we may have to catch a later train and –'

'It is very kind of your grandfather to take such an interest in his grandson's education.'

'My grandfather pays for my schooling, miss,' I said. 'He has always taken a special interest in my education. He had an unfortunate experience as a schoolboy and it affected him deeply.'

'Really?' she said.

'He was at a school where there was a terrible incident involving one of the boys.'

'How awful,' said the Woman in White. 'Do tell.'

'Well,' I said, trying to ignore the grin she now wore and determined to wipe it from her face. 'Actually, there was a suicide.'

She raised an eyebrow but said nothing.

'I'm sorry if that shocks you.' I hoped very much that it had. 'But I'm afraid that was what happened. And I'm afraid it gets much, much worse.'

'Go on,' she said.

'It concerns the headmaster of my grandfather's school. The boys called him Monty. His real name was Montague –'

'And what did this Monty do?' she interrupted.

'He put it about that a certain boy was stealing things from the other boys. This lad was already unpopular and they needed no further encouragement to attack the poor soul and beat him mercilessly.'

The Woman in White looked singularly unimpressed and so I felt I needed to get to the point of the tale.

'That hardly seems extraordinary, I know,' I said. 'Boys are often beaten at school, by other boys and by the teachers. But this was different. The beatings went on and on and became more and more vicious with each new theft. And, of course, there was the boy's innocence to take into consideration.'

'He was innocent?' she asked in a curious voice, as if she already knew the answer.

'Yes,' I said. 'And what is more, it was the headmaster –'

'Montague,' she said.

'Yes,' I said, annoyed by the interruption. 'It was he who had stolen all the things. The boy was blameless.'

'And this boy committed suicide,' she said, 'before the headmaster's crime was discovered?'

'Yes,' I said. Why did she insist upon ruining my

telling of the story? 'My grandfather was so upset by this that he was determined that none of his children or grandchildren should ever be subjected to such treatment.'

'He felt guilty?' she asked with a smile.

'I cannot see what reason he would have to feel guilty,' I said, though I had wondered this myself many times.

'Because he was one of the boys who beat that poor unfortunate soul and drove him to suicide,' she said.

'I find it offensive that you would suggest that,' I protested.

'But in your heart you have always felt it to be true, haven't you?'

She reached over and touched my hand. In the instant that she did so, I was transported, as if in a dream, to another place, to a room I did not recognise – and yet, as with a dream, I knew exactly where I was.

I stood at one end of a school dormitory, looking along a row of beds to where a group of boys were gathered in front of another lad who was pleading his innocence to them. A boy stepped forward from the pack and punched him hard in the stomach, making him groan and collapse to the floor, where the same boy led a vicious bout of kicking and stamping. Despite my only having seen him as an old man, I somehow knew this boy to be grandfather.

'How?' was all I could say to her when the vision faded and I found myself once more in the railway carriage.

'You've had a moment of revelation, that is all,' she said. 'But you should sleep now. You look so tired.'

I was beyond tiredness. I was like a somnambulist, more asleep than awake. I began to wonder if all of this – the Woman in White, the train journey, my sleeping fellow passengers – were not itself part of a dream and I had yet to leave my bed.

'Could you not tell me one more story?' I said, for I wanted something on which to concentrate. Dream or no dream, I had the strongest feeling that I should not let myself fall into that deep slumber that seemed to await me like the blackness of a bottomless pit.

10

A CRACK IN
THE WALL

Philip stood with his mother in the large empty
room that was to be his bedroom. It was an attic
room, with the ceiling sloping down almost to the
floor on one side and a dormer window giving
views of the cherry tree lined crescent below.

'Oh dear me, no,' said his mother, tapping her
hands together in a swift patter. 'This wallpaper
will have to go. Look at it: that ghastly yellow tinge.
It is enough to send someone out of their wits. I
shall have Benson and his fellows remove it
immediately.'

Philip rather liked the wallpaper, but he knew

better than to get involved in matters of interior decor, which was undisputedly his mother's domain.

In fact, so obsessed had she become with it that Philip's father had commented more than once that the sole reason for moving to this new house in Chelsea was because Philip's mother had run out of ideas for their old home.

For as long as Philip could remember, there had been a continual procession of decorators in and out of the house, as well as delivery men bringing the latest fashion in pots and rugs and furniture, while removal men arrived to take away the previous year's fashion.

But though Philip had not wanted to move, he was forced to admit that the new house was far better than their old one, bigger and grander and on a much nicer street. And more to the point, his room was bigger and grander too.

And so workmen were duly instructed to come and rid Philip's bedroom-to-be of its yellow wallpaper and replace it with something of his mother's choosing.

Mr Benson was a tall and well-built man, with close-cropped hair and small piercing eyes, set deep in a wide and powerful face.

He had a boy called Tommy working with him, a gangly, jug-eared lad of about fifteen or so, Philip guessed, with a habit of coughing slightly before he said anything.

For all his effusive 'Yes, madam's and 'Of course, madam's, Philip could tell from his bearing that Benson was a man for whom servility did not come naturally. He noticed that the ingratiating smile left Benson's lips the instant his mother's back was turned, and saw the quick roll of the eyes at his mother's more outlandish requests.

While the work was going on, Philip was forced to sleep in a guest room that his mother had already decorated in a particularly gross and feminine fashion, with not a surface left free of ornamention of some sort or another. He could not move for ceramic vases and peacock feathers, and so had a special interest in seeing that his attic room was completed with the utmost haste.

As soon as he was washed and dressed and breakfasted, Philip would go and stand in the doorway, checking on the workmen's progress as they stripped the wallpaper from the walls and began to repair and redecorate.

His first visits had been greeted by warm hellos from man and boy, and with hair ruffles and winks from Benson. But with each successive visit, the greetings had become less and less enthusiastic, until a kind of stand-off had occurred, with Philip making his impatience and disappointment in their slow progress quite as obvious as Benson's resentment of being watched over.

Benson tried to intimidate Philip into leaving them alone, but Philip was not easily intimidated. Every now and then, Benson would give Philip a look that made it clear that he would have liked to cuff the boy round the ear and send him sprawling, just as Philip had seen him do once with the gormless Tommy. But still Philip kept his vigil at the doorway. He was keenly aware that there was little the man could do or complain about, as Philip always took great pains never to actually get in their way.

'For the love of –' said Tommy one bright morning, the sun sending a golden beam through the dormer window and lighting up a strip of the bare floorboards.

'What's up, Tommy?' said Benson.

'It's this crack here, Mr Benson,' said Tommy despairingly. 'I've tried everything to fill it but it just won't stick. Every time I fills it, it just pops out and falls on the floor. I don't know what to try next.'

'Don't get yourself all het up about it, Tommy,' said Benson, giving the boy a kindly pat on the shoulder. 'Leave it with me. You're probably making your filler a bit too wet. Or too dry. Who knows? I'll sort it out. There's plenty of other stuff to be getting on with.'

Philip watched from the doorway. Benson saw him and gave him a wink. *He's in a good mood today*, thought Philip. Benson set about mixing up some filler on a small palette, whistling a jaunty tune as he did so; then he began to fill the crack. Philip stepped forward to have a better look.

'There now,' said Benson. 'That ain't so bad now, is it, young master?'

'Will it fall off like before?' asked Philip.

'Fall off?' said Benson with a sniff. 'I think I knows how to fill a bit of cracked plaster after thirty-odd years doing it.'

'Sorry,' said Philip, sensing he had offended the man.

'That's all right,' he said. 'I takes a lot of pride in what I do.'

Philip nodded.

'It's too easy just to slap things up like they do

today. You see them old churches and big houses and such. Just you look at the craftsmanship there. You don't get that these days, I'll tell you straight. These youngsters ain't got the patience.'

'Like Tommy, you mean,' said Philip.

Benson frowned and squinted at him.

'Tommy's all right,' said Benson. 'I ain't saying nothing about Tommy. He tries his best. He's had a hard life too, though you never hears him complain.'

Again, Philip could tell he had caused offence, though he was not altogether sure why.

'Sorry,' he said again.

'You're a right one for the sorrys, ain't you,' said Benson, his eyes cold despite the smile.

When Philip returned after lunch and peeped round the doorway he saw that Benson's cheerful mood had evaporated. He was down on his haunches. The crack was back.

'I don't believe it,' said Benson, picking up one of the larger pieces of filler lying on the floor.

'That's just the same as what happened to me,' said Tommy.

'It don't make sense,' said Benson, getting up and peering at the crack resentfully. 'It's almost like something's pushing the filler out.'

'What we going to do, Mr Benson?' said Tommy. 'It'll probably fall out again, won't it?'

Benson sighed and nodded.

'It does seem so, Tommy boy,' he said. He looked round and Philip ducked back behind the wall, worried that he had been seen, but Benson was merely being cautious.

'Here's what we're going to do, lad,' he said, pulling Tommy closer. 'We're going to paper over it.'

'Paper over it?' repeated Tommy, a trace of admonishment in his voice.

'That's right,' said Benson a little more forcefully. 'These spoilt toffs here won't know the difference, will they? They'll stick a bloody great painting over it and never know there was ever a problem. And if they ever do find it, who's to say there hasn't been some kind of subsidence or something?'

'Subsidence?' repeated Tommy.

'Exactly,' said Benson, ruffling his hair. 'Loads of it round here. It's the river, you see. Wet clay and all that. We'll get this papering done first thing tomorrow before any of them spots it and makes us fill the damned thing again.'

Philip smiled to himself, remembering Benson's speech about the rise of shoddy workmanship.

What a fraud he was. There was always something satisfying about catching adults in a web of their own pomposity, and Philip savoured the moment – right up until the workmen's footsteps began to head his way and Philip had to scamper down the hall as quickly and as quietly as possible.

Philip stood in the deserted room and tried to take possession of it. He knew that it would be his room, that in reality it was already his room, but it didn't feel like that.

Empty of furniture, stripped of wallpaper and carpet, it seemed like an empty vessel waiting to be claimed by anyone who so chose.

Philip shuffled round in a circle, taking in the whole room. And as he turned, he noticed the crack in the wall that had so confounded the workmen.

Philip walked hesitantly over to it, a floorboard creaking plaintively as he did so.

He stood about a foot away from the wall and, after a pause in which he had to resist the impulse to turn and walk away, he leaned forward and peered into the crack. There was something in there.

Philip tried to poke his finger in, but the gap was too narrow. He looked round and saw that Benson had left a bag of nails by the door, so he picked one up and returned to the crack in the plaster.

A few seconds of exploration with the point of the nail and out tumbled a tiny folded-up piece of what he at first took to be paper but, as he opened it, realised was probably parchment.

It was covered in strange markings and symbols. Down one side there was something he presumed to be writing, though it was in a language and a script he did not recognise.

Why someone would have placed the parchment in a crack in the wall was a total mystery to him. But Philip rather liked mysteries.

As he looked up from the parchment he had the distinct impression that he had detected move-ment, though for a moment he could not think from where. Then Philip leaned forward until his eyelashes brushed against the tattered edge of the crack.

Was it his imagination? No, no, he was sure of it. There was something there. His eyes slowly grew accustomed to the gloom. There was another room through the crack. He could just detect the far wall of a room that looked to be a mirror of the one in which he stood.

But even as his eyes confirmed this to be the

case, his mind told him that it was an impossibility. He stepped back and tried to make sense of it, but he could not.

His room was at the gable end of the house. The wall with the crack was an outside wall; the house was detached. There was nothing beyond it save an alleyway leading to a coach house that stood in the shade of a large plane tree. Just as he became entangled in these conflicting realities, something seemed to flicker past the crack.

Philip hesistated, then leaned tentatively forward, peering in, but though the room remained, all was still. He stepped forward, pressing his face against the wall again, and squinted into the crevice.

He had hoped that greater scrutiny would reveal this room to be an illusion, a trick of his imagination; but far from it. He could see very clearly now that, however impossible it seemed to be, there was a room beyond that wall and, moreover, there was someone in it.

Standing at the far side of the room was a tall, thin figure dressed in black, with his back to Philip, almost as if he too were inspecting a crack in the wall at that end of the room.

Philip gasped, and at the sound of his voice the

man in black began to turn round, slowly, hesitat-ingly. Philip's heart was thumping at his ribs like a bare-knuckle boxer, but he felt compelled to watch.

The man faced him, but Philip could not make out the features of that face. A shadow covered the upper part of his torso, though what was casting it was a mystery. It was almost as if he carried his own shadow with him. He stood, his head tilted slightly as if listening, his hands twitching. Then suddenly he began to walk with great purpose straight towards Philip, who pushed himself away from the wall. As soon as did so, he backed straight into someone and yelled out in panic.

'Well now,' said a voice behind him. 'What's all this?'

Philip pointed towards the wall but, try as he might, he couldn't quite make his mouth form the words he wanted.

'Th-th-there's s-someone there!' he blurted out at last.

Tommy snorted.

'Where?' said Benson. 'What are you talking about? Are you all right, young fellow?'

'On the other side of the wall,' said Philip, feeling a bit stronger now that Benson was at his side. 'You can see him through the crack.'

Benson looked at the floor beneath the crack and saw the pieces of plaster that had fallen when Philip had pulled the parchment free.

'That's not very helpful, is it now?' said Benson coldly. 'There's enough of a crack there without you giving it a helping hand. I suppose you think that's amusing, eh? To make us poor folk have to work a little harder?'

'But the other side . . .'

'There ain't nothing on the other side of that wall but stinking London air,' said Benson crossly. 'Tommy, mix up some paste and get a roll of that paper. Let's make a start on the room, shall we, before this young fellow brings the whole place down upon our heads.'

'Shouldn't you fill that hole first?' said Philip.

Benson put one of his great hands on Philip's shoulder and eased him firmly out of the room.

'You run along now,' he said, 'and leave us to work, there's a good lad.'

Then he gave Philip a shove – a hard shove – and turned back to the room.

Philip's mother was a little surprised when Philip told her he was never going to sleep in the room he had seemed so keen on and was determined to remain in the guest room, despite all his previous complaints.

She was also annoyed to hear that he insisted they move at the first opportunity because the house was haunted. Letting out a series of escalating sighs, she had listened to some nonsense about a crack in the wall and something the boy claimed to have seen through it.

Philip's mother had always found children and their overactive imaginations alarming, and it had taken all of her husband's persuasive powers to convince her that they should have one of their own. She was, therefore, relieved when her son turned out to be refreshingly unimaginative. This new change in his character was disturbing.

Philip's father said that the best thing to do was simply to switch the rooms. If Philip did not want that room, then it could become the guest room. Philip could stay where he was and they could just change the decor of his room to something more suitable. As he pointed out, the room that was to have been Philip's was larger, and so there really was not a problem.

Philip no longer stood in the doorway to the room in which Benson and Tommy worked, but hurried past instead, both to avoid a glimpse of the dreaded wall and its sinister fissure, and to avoid any comment from Benson, who clearly enjoyed the boy's discomfort.

Benson eventually hung a door on the bedroom and so the work went on unseen. Philip would sometimes pause in the hall and stare at the door, at the light that leaked out from underneath.

Without the attentions of Philip or their employers, Benson and Tommy finished the room in no time at all and moved on to the entrance hall and staircase, as Philip's mother had instructed.

Philip had been standing in the upstairs hallway as the men moved their equipment out of the room and cleared away. Tommy gave Philip a wink. They left the door open. Philip hesitated and then, curiosity overwhelming his fear, stepped inside.

He stood in the newly papered and painted room, the sun streaming in and lighting up a floating galaxy of dust particles. The room was so utterly transformed from when he had last seen it that it felt like a different room altogether.

He knew that the crack must still be there under the layer of wallpaper, but it did not feel like it was there. It was as if the crack had never existed and so it was as though the room beyond it had never existed, nor its mysterious occupant. It was as if the whole thing had been a crack in his mind, a fissure in his imagination.

Philip would still never have wanted to sleep in that room, but it was surprisingly easy just to stand there. He grinned, pleased at having overcome his dread of the place.

The door slammed shut behind him and he ran to open it. He tried the doorknob but it was as if someone was holding it from the other side; it did not budge.

'Mr Benson!' shouted Philip, for he felt sure that was who it was. 'Please – let me out!'

There was no reply. He tugged again but to no avail.

'Tommy!' he shouted. 'Is that you? Please let me out. Please!'

But again, there was no reply. Philip took a deep breath and tried to be as quiet as possible. He hoped that whoever it was might think he had let go and relax their grip. He was about to give the doorknob a sudden yank, when he became aware of a noise behind him.

At first he couldn't locate where the noise was coming from. Whatever it was, it sounded as though it was moving. But where? The room was empty.

He tried the door handle again but it was still jammed. He called out again, but no one came. The noise was getting louder. He wondered if it might be a mouse under the floorboards or up in the roof, but rejected this idea as soon as it was formed. The sound was not one of scampering feet. It was a slithering sound.

Then he saw it: an almost imperceptible movement out of the corner of his eye. He peered, trying to see what it was, but there was nothing there but the wall and the wallpaper. Then it moved again.

There was something under the wallpaper. It was hard to make out, but there it was – a definite and unmistakable ripple in the pattern, a ripple that was moving, and moving swiftly, across the wall.

Philip watched the thing swimming beneath the surface of the paper, mesmerised by the undulating pattern and fearfully, but hypnotically, fascinated by the nature of this unseen, unknown thing. What, he wondered breathlessly, could it be?

But even as he wondered this, Philip knew that it had something to do with the crack in the wall and the man – whoever he was. And sure enough, the rippling began to move in circles around that spot, circles that decreased in diameter at each rotation until eventually it sat quivering, its size and shape exactly mirroring the jagged hole beneath.

Philip was being pulled in two directions: his body wanted to run – to at least hurl himself to the farthest corner of the room and away from that thing. It was as if the fibres of his muscles instinctively knew they had to carry Philip out of harm's way. His brain, too, fizzed and crackled with fear and dread.

But something else was keeping him rooted to the spot. It was some other part of Philip that pulsed with curiosity, with fascination – with desire. While every cell in his body, every jangling nerve, urged him to run, this hunger to know the power he could feel beyond that skin of patterned paper was irresistible.

He reached out a hand and touched the paper. The ripple seemed merely like a bubble left behind when the paper had been hung. Philip took hold of it between his fingernails and ripped it, letting the torn fragment fall to the floor.

He leaned forward, his heart pounding. The crack in the wall was no longer dark. A strange blue light emanated from it and Philip felt pulled towards its glow.

He looked through and there, once again, was the room. It was bathed in the same dull blue glow that lit Philip's wide eye as it peered through the crack.

The room looked deserted now: a tattered, shabby, blank version of the room in which Philip stood. Then suddenly the man appeared, blocking out the room entirely, his wild, bloodshot eye only inches away from Philip's.

Philip recoiled as if he had been shot, falling backwards and scrabbling away to the other side of the room, staring back at the rip in the wallpaper and the crack, now dark once more, deep and dark like a wound. The doorknob rattled and the door swung open. Philip screamed.

Benson walked into the room.

'And what are you up to, eh?' he said. He leaned forward. Philip could smell beer on his breath.

'Nothing,' said Philip. 'I was just looking.'

'Thought you was scared of this room, little man,' said Benson with a leering grin. 'Thought you said there was a ghostie in here.'

Philip was staring at the other end of the room and Benson followed his gaze. He saw the ripped wallpaper and cursed under his breath.

'Why don't you run along, eh?' hissed Benson between clenched teeth. 'Ain't you got something better to be doing than making extra work for me?

I suppose you think it's funny, do you? That your idea of a lark then, is it? Off with you before I –'

Benson lifted his hand as though he was going to strike, but though Philip flinched, the blow never came. Benson might have been a bit drunk, but he wasn't stupid.

Philip took the opportunity to scramble to his feet. He stood staring at Benson and was filled with a sudden loathing for the man. How horrible he was, thought Philip. He was such a bully, such a brute. Someone ought to teach him a lesson.

Benson's eyes suddenly widened in horror and he backed away from Philip, his hands out-stretched. He was mumbling to himself. Tears started rolling down his cheeks. He looked like an enormous baby. Philip could not help but laugh, as he followed him out of the room into the corridor.

When Benson got to the stairwell, a new calm seemed to come over him. He sat on the banister, put first one leg and then the other, over it, and took one last look at Philip before falling forward, head first, on to the marble floor below.

The sound of Benson's head hitting the marble was unlike any Philip had ever heard before. It was followed rapidly by shouts from Tommy and hysterical screaming from the parlour maid.

The expression on Benson's face before he jumped had seemed to say, 'Must I?' It was the look of someone whose will was broken, of someone who had no choice but to obey. It was the look of a dog beaten into submission. It was an expression Philip had rather enjoyed.

The commotion from downstairs grew in intensity, with footsteps clattering about in the hall. Philip heard someone take a few steps up the stairs, then go back down again. He saw no reason why he should get involved. He had never liked Benson, after all.

He suddenly felt an odd twinge in his head – not quite pain, or, if it was pain, a strange, almost pleasurable one, like the feeling of ears popping. He went to his bedroom and looked in the mirror on his wardrobe.

There was something different about Philip's face. He could not have said what it was exactly, but he looked changed in some subtle way.

He felt different too. Again, he would have struggled to say how. He was not ill, but he felt odd. He felt as if he were suddenly not large enough to contain all that was within him. He felt constrained by the limitations of his own body.

Philip knew that something, someone, other

than himself now inhabited his body. But instead of feeling horror at this parasite within, he experienced a strange sense of completeness. He accepted the presence willingly – more than willingly. He wanted it. He wanted it. More than anything in the world.

11

THE TUNNEL'S MOUTH

I slumped sideways at the end of the tale, as if I'd
been held in the talons of some huge beast – a
beast such as had leapt from the confines of the
barrow to catch those two unfortunate brothers.
But unlike that one, my imaginary beast had loosed
its grip.

The images were vivid as always, however unwel-
come. I saw the dark man lunging towards the
crack in the wall, I saw the broken-headed Benson
lying in a pool of his own blood, and again I saw a
flickering something lurking just out of sight.

I felt utterly compelled to listen to this woman's

stories, but wondered if I would have the strength to hear another, for each one had sapped yet more of my energy, so that now it took a force of will to keep my eyes open.

The strangeness of this last tale seemed particularly to stay with me and I now had the hardest job in ridding my mind of the fevered imaginings it inspired: of that demon the boy had become possessed by. I felt convinced that should I allow my eyes to close, I might find myself in that awful other room.

Outside, darkness had deepened and some of its chill was seeping through the glass and the fabric of the carriage; I shivered at its touch. The light seemed to be draining from the sky. Night was coming.

The Woman in White sat back in her seat, watching me with her usual inscrutable intensity. Her image was smudged now by my tired eyes, and she was becoming as blurred as her reflection in the compartment window.

I tried in vain to marshal my brain and bully it into a more disciplined state. How long had we been sitting here? How long had my companions been asleep? I tapped the Bishop on the arm. Nothing.

'Sir?' I said.

He slept on. I gave him a shove. Still no reaction. I clapped my hands loudly. None of the sleepers so much as twitched. The Woman in White smiled.

A horrible thought now occurred to me. Perhaps this strange woman had drugged my companions. Or, if not drugged them, then affected them in some way as yet unknown to me.

At the same music hall I mentioned earlier, I saw a man perform a startling feat of mental wizardry known as hypnotism. The man – Mesmero was his name – stood at the edge of the stage in the glare of the limelight, peering out unblinkingly. Then, with an almost supernatural hold over members of the audience, he encouraged people to behave in the most comical ways. By turns they were encouraged to bark like dogs, roll on the floor like infants in a tantrum or cavort like drunken sailors. One of our number was invited onstage and was made to fall asleep in an instant. Did this woman possess a similar gift? Had she hypnotised us?

Perhaps she was even a murderess – such women did exist, I knew. Perhaps she had in some way delivered a poison to each of us in turn. And maybe, because of my youth, my resistance to it was stronger than that of my older fellow passengers.

Had they already succumbed to its deadly effects? Perhaps the poison had yet to reach its fatal climax.

This theory, however disturbing, would certainly explain her reticence in telling me her name and would account in some small degree for her peculiar manner.

'I fear that something untoward has happened here,' I said, looking at her all the time. Did I have enough strength to get to the door? I could use the surgeon's briefcase to break the glass. Maybe the door would open from the other side.

'Really?' she murmured.

'Yes,' I said. 'It can scarcely be normal for these men to have slept so soundly for so long.' I clapped my hands and stamped my feet loudly. 'Do you see?' I shouted, my voice cracking. 'Nothing rouses them.'

I made no attempt to disguise the accusatory tone I knew was in my voice. I would not sit here quietly and simply let this woman work her evil on me. I was my father's son, after all.

'You seem very excitable suddenly,' she said.

And I *wonder that you are so calm,* I thought to myself, straining to remain fully awake. I *wonder why it is that you are not more concerned about the state*

248

of these men, or why it is that we have sat in this train for goodness knows how long, with no word from anyone to tell us what is happening.

The Woman in White smiled at me, and then looked out of the window seemingly without a care in the world.

'And where has all this wondering got you?' she said.

I frowned, unable in that instant to recall whether or not I had spoken my thoughts aloud.

'I do not know,' I answered. I didn't have the courage to accuse her directly of any crime without the evidence to substantiate it.

I took out my watch and remembered that it had stopped. I shook it angrily and stood up to try the window once more, but it was still jammed. I banged on it angrily and leaned forward, grabbing the Farmer by the lapels of his coat and shaking him. He did not stir.

'Calm yourself,' said the Woman in White.

'Calm yourself, you say?' I shouted hysterically. 'I think I've been calm long enough! What's wrong with these men? What have you done to them?'

'Done to them?' she said, looking a little hurt. 'You blame me for their condition?'

'I . . . I . . . I think I do,' I spluttered.

'I assure you that I am not responsible,' she said. 'Please, sit down.'

As soon as she said the words I felt as though my legs would not support me and it was all I could do to reach my seat before falling to the floor. I cursed my weakness and summoned up one last burst of energy to confront her and assert myself.

'Miss, I must insist you tell me the time,' I said, trying to think how I might gainfully proceed from here. Perhaps she had a gun in her bag. I was convinced now that I was dealing with someone who would stop at nothing to achieve whatever twisted goal she sought. What would Sherlock Holmes have done in my circumstances? I wondered.

'The time?' she asked with a smile.

'Yes!' I said loudly, hoping to show that I was made of sterner stuff than she may have imagined. I was pleased to see that this forcefulness had some effect. She looked at her watch and nodded to herself.

'Why, it is *your* time, Robert,' she said.

'What do you mean?' I said in exasperation.

To my utter astonishment, she leaned across the carriage, grabbed my necktie and, before I quite knew what she was doing, she had pulled my face towards hers.

We kissed. But this was not the gentle kiss I had shared with Chastity Manningtree, sheltering in the gazebo at my cousin's wedding in the summer. This was not a shared kiss.

She placed her free hand at the back of my head and thrust me into her face with a force and passion I would scarcely have believed a woman could possess.

I struggled. I am sure I struggled. And yet there was something overpowering, something intoxicating, about her embrace. I felt myself falling as if from a great height into a mist-shrouded valley far below.

I cannot say how long I fell or how long I would have continued to fall, but I was suddenly interrupted, snatched from this dream-like descent and hauled back.

Instead of the soft lips of the storyteller against my mouth, I now felt an altogether different sensation. My eyes snapped open. A strange face was clamped to mine and I struggled free, gasping and coughing.

'What on earth?!' I spluttered, staring at the mustachioed man who, moments before, had seemingly been kissing me. I could see quite clearly now that he wore the black tunic and brass buttons of a police constable. But I struggled to comprehend the meaning of these things.

'George here has saved your life, lad,' said a second man I had not noticed until then but who was similarly attired and therefore also a policeman. 'You was a goner for sure.'

I stared at them in horror and confusion.

'Mouth to mouth, they calls it,' said the first policeman. I spat one of his moustache hairs from my mouth and looked about me, the sounds and smells of the area now flooding in.

In my confused state I wondered if I had not died and gone to hell. And if this was the case, I wished that I had been allowed more opportunities to sin, for this seemed a rather excessive judgement on what had been a frankly dull and blameless life. But I was not dead. I could see that now.

I had awoken to a scene that could have come from Mr Wells' *The War of the Worlds*. The train lay on its side like a dead animal, smashed and twisted, split open, gored. All around, people were shouting and calling for help.

With a jarring metal-on-metal screech, parts of the wreckage were pulled apart or dragged aside. Everywhere there were percussive clangs and clatters, the shattering of glass, the splintering of wood.

My eyes needed more time to adjust to the

darkness, for the sun had now dropped out of sight behind the hill through which the tunnel had been bored and, though there was a glow in the west, it was faint and eerie. Lanterns and torches moved this way and that like fireflies amid the gloom and the chaos.

'I don't understand,' I said, my voice sounding dry and cracked.

'You've been in a train wreck, son,' said one of the policemen. 'A terrible one. You was lucky.'

I did not feel especially lucky. I suddenly remembered the others in my compartment and tried to sit upright, wincing with pain at the effort and sinking back down breathlessly.

'There were other passengers,' I hissed. 'Others in my compartment.'

The two men exchanged a glance.

'There was a young lady dressed in white, a man of the cloth, another who –'

One of them leaned forward and patted me on the shoulder.

'Like I said,' he murmured. 'You was lucky.'

I looked from face to face and back towards the scene of chaos and destruction. Their meaning was clear to me even in my confused state, but I couldn't quite come to terms with it. Was I really the sole survivor from that compartment?

'Your mother'll be pleased to see you, at any rate,' said one of the policemen. 'She's been up there waiting for –'

'She's not my . . .'

But I could not finish the sentence.

'What was that, son?' he said.

'Nothing,' I replied.

For, strange to say, I wanted nothing more at that moment than to see a familiar face. I'm not ashamed to admit that tears now sprang to my eyes. The first policeman put a comforting hand on my shoulder.

'She's been out of her mind with worry. We've kept everyone back, but there don't seem to be too much wrong with you. I think we can get you to her soon enough.'

I began now to become more aware of what was going on in the dark around us. Rescuers were moving about the scene, occasionally obscured by drifting smoke. Injured people were whimpering. A woman was crying hysterically. There was an acrid smell in the air. A small fire burned near the tunnel's mouth and made its depths all the darker.

But it was by this firelight, in fact, that I saw her: the woman from the carriage, the Woman in White,

254

the storyteller. I gasped and grinned.

How incredible, I thought, that she should have escaped from the wreck utterly unharmed, not only unharmed but unblemished, her white clothes still unmarked and gleaming bright against the darkness. It was a miracle.

I was pleased, too, to see that with her were the other occupants of our carriage: the Major, the Farmer, the Bishop, the Surgeon. They were also unharmed, it seemed. There were others there I did not know, gathered in a group beside her.

The policeman was obviously misinformed, and I was very pleased that he was. These people stood apart, no doubt allowing the injured to be treated without obstruction. Far from being the sole survivor, by some freak of misfortune it looked as though I was the only one in our compartment who had come to any harm.

But then, as I looked away, I saw a stretcher being carried past me up the steep zigzag path of the embankment, the bearers struggling to find their footing and skidding to a halt. The body they bore was one of the accident's fatalities, a blanket covering the head, and as the bearers slipped, so too did the blanket, and the face was uncovered only inches from mine.

It was horribly torn and beaten about, but through the blood and bruises I was able to discern the features of the Major I could somehow still see, standing in his unharmed form, at the tunnel's mouth.

A terrible pain gripped my heart and I hissed and sank back. The Woman in White took some hurried steps towards me, moving with a ghastly, flickering speed. There was a fire burning between us, but the resulting heat haze did not altogether account for the strange, blurred quality of her approach. She stretched out an arm towards me, and her grasping fingers seemed to be the only things in sharp focus.

Suddenly air rushed into my lungs and life back into my limbs and her arm dropped to her side. Her shimmering, distorted face stared at me for a moment and then she retreated back towards the tunnel in the same odd, jerking manner in which she had advanced. How could I ever have thought that face to be beautiful?

I saw everything clearly now. That outstretched, clutching hand had awakened some long dormant memory. She was the mysterious woman from the riverbank all those years ago when I had nearly drowned.

But she had been no guardian angel. She was not trying to help me at all. She had been trying to claim me as she had claimed the lives of my fellow passengers.

She was the thing that remained forever unseen in my visions of her tales. She lurked near the bodies of those whose lives were so cruelly taken. She was there always, waiting.

As the stretcher bearers lifted me up, I saw her rejoining the others. She turned once and smiled back at me, then turned again, shepherding the dead into the dreadful, unbounded and unending darkness of that tunnel.

READ ON
(IF YOU DARE)
FOR A SPINE-TINGLING
BONUS STORY

12

THE REST CURE

I think I was delivered from that awful catastrophe
a wiser and better young man than I had been on
boarding that railway carriage.

My injuries – my physical ones, at least – were
minor ones. I did suffer a mental breakdown for a
while and had a brief stay in a grim institution for
those suffering from various maladies of the mind.
I hated it there. I knew I didn't belong when I
found myself in the garden one day, sitting alongside a wretch who had poisoned his own children.

I was so grateful to be reunited with my stepmother. I am not ashamed to say that I allowed her

to embrace me as one would a small child, or that, like a small child, I sobbed my heart out in gratitude for my deliverance, in shame at my treatment of this blameless woman and for a great many things besides.

My grandfather agreed that I should stay with my stepmother for a while, as I was not well enough to start school. He said that I would need time to convalesce, and though I had initially thought that I might spend this period with him, I was pleased that I now had a chance to get to know my stepmother better. I had the distinct impression that my grandfather did not want to be burdened with me.

In any event, my stepmother had already formulated a plan. She told me of a cottage that she had inherited – it was the house she grew up in. She had not been able to part with it and rented it out. However, the tenants had recently moved out and the property was now empty.

My stepmother suggested that this cottage, in a quiet part of rural Cambridgeshire, would be a perfect place for me to recuperate. I was happy to agree.

And so I found myself on another train. My stepmother had been keen to find an alternative mode of transport, but it was my belief that if you fell from a horse you should lose no time in getting back on. I thought that if I did not get into a railway carriage soon, I might never be able to.

To be sure, it was perhaps the most difficult thing I had ever done, setting that first foot in the carriage doorway, and the compartment itself was horribly similar to the one in which I had sat with the Woman in White.

But though I could never have thought it possible, the fact that my stepmother now occupied her space seemed to work as a cure, and the pain and fear faded.

Having said that, I was heartily glad for the absence of tunnels on our route. I was not yet ready for them. I think I should have collapsed in panic. I'm sure I would have, in fact. I am horribly sure.

It was a pleasant day, if a cold one. The views became wider and more expansive as we approached Cambridge and this had a similar effect on my spirits. I was not quite happy as yet, but I did feel my mood lighten.

We changed at Cambridge to a branch line and continued our journey. We appeared to be the only people in the entire carriage, but my stepmother assured me that in summer the train could be unbearably crowded. It was hard to imagine.

Before long we alighted once again at a small station and from there walked the mile or so to my stepmother's cottage. There was a chill in the air and it was good to find that the housekeeper had lit fires in all the hearths.

The housekeeper, who lived nearby, also doubled as our cook and set a hearty stew on the table for us, followed by a delicious apple pie. I don't think I had ever eaten so much in my life.

We retired to the lounge and the fire, and the housekeeper popped in to tell us she was leaving and that her daughter would be in first thing in the morning to refresh the fires and prepare our breakfast.

It was dark now but still early. We were both tired from our journey, but neither of us so exhausted that we were quite ready for our beds.

'Perhaps I could tell you a story?' my stepmother suggested, as we sat gazing into the fire.

This was a rather startling proposal given my experience on the train, but my stepmother was not to know that. We may have become closer, but there was no way that I could tell her or anyone else what had happened that day. It was hard enough for me to accept it.

'The night is young and the firelight conducive, is it not?' she added.

'*Conducive*? Is it a ghost story, then?' I asked.

'Not exactly,' she said. 'But a strange one all the same. Do you have a taste for tales of the supernatural, Robert?'

My mouth felt suddenly rather dry.

'I used to,' I replied.

'Used to?'

'Forgive me,' I said with a weak smile. I didn't want to do anything to harm the new state of friendship between us. 'I still do. Please – tell me your story. I'm sure I will enjoy it.'

'Very well, then,' she said, settling back into the Windsor chair with a creak. 'If you're sure . . .'

'Quite sure,' I said.

THE VOICE

This story concerns a girl – let us call her Dora –
who, very sadly, found herself motherless at the
tender age of thirteen.

Dora had been very close to her mother, who was
young and of a girlish disposition. They had
seemed more like sisters.

They both loved to ride and were very experienced, but even the most experienced rider can fall.
When her mother fell from the saddle one day as
they cantered along the green lane near the river,
she did irreparable damage to her insides. She died
after days of morphine-addled agony. Dora had not

ridden since and the very sight of a horse caused her to weep inconsolably.

Dora's father decided it would be best to move out of the family home, where there were so many memories. Dora would have dearly loved to stay there for ever but she knew she couldn't. Her father saw to it that the house was rented out.

While he did his best to comfort his daughter, he had never seen the sense in riding for pleasure, and the accident only served to confirm this opinion. In truth, he had found his wife's girlish reckless-ness more and more irritating over the years and he was unable to grieve as deeply as he felt he ought.

Being, essentially, a good man, this inability caused him considerable anguish. The only person who seemed to understand what he was going through was a widow who lived nearby, who confessed to a similar shortfall of grief when her husband had shot himself in the neck while clean-ing a shotgun.

To the consternation of neighbours and the bit-ter sadness and fury of Dora, her father and the widow married less than a year after her mother's death.

Dora was, by turns, coldly indifferent and openly hostile to this interloper. Her father appeared unperturbed about this at first but, as time went on, some latent feeling of guilt or remorse made him ever more desirous of his daughter's approval.

Though he often took Dora's side in her frequent disputes with her stepmother, his wife was always able to work on him once they were alone, and he would eventually sidle up to Dora and ask her to be kinder to her new mother, for his sake.

And so the weeks turned into months. Dora's view of her stepmother did not change and certainly did not improve, but she felt less and less inclined to provoke her. She felt less inclined to consider her at all.

This stand-off persisted until, one day, Dora allowed herself to be persuaded to accompany her father and stepmother on a walk to a local beauty spot.

A short carriage ride away from where they lived was a valley which rose steeply on one side. A walk through woods took one up and along a precipice and allowed for spectacular views of the surrounding countryside.

Picnics were often enjoyed at the summit of the hill, but this was October and, though a fine morning, it was cold enough for scarves and gloves.

The unlikely threesome set out. The atmosphere

was not exactly jovial but, considering everything, it was cordial enough. Dora's father was in particularly high spirits.

When they reached the start of the wooded walk, Dora's father passed through the kissing gate and immediately turned to wait for his wife. To Dora's intense embarrassment they made a great show of kissing before he opened the gate to let her through.

Dora could not stop herself from sighing rather more loudly than she had intended. Her father and stepmother turned to look at her, both with the same withering expression. That was when she heard the voice in her head.

Enough, it said. *She has to go.*

Dora was shocked at the tone of the voice. It wasn't that she had never thought such a thing about her stepmother before, only it had never been with such brazen malice.

Wait until the top of the climb, said the voice. *Then just one little push. That's all it will take.*

Dora's breath shortened and her heart raced. Her father and stepmother continued on their way along the path that led to the foot of the hill. A wood of oak and hazel soon engulfed them as the path began to wind its way up.

Keep together, said the voice. *Stay close.*

The climb was steep in places and Dora's shoes were pinching. She had been determined at least to look more elegant than her stepmother, but she wished now that she had chosen something a little more practical.

She had always loved this walk – it had been a favourite of her mother's – but that association now took a good deal of the pleasure away. How she missed her poor mother. How she wished she were here instead of –

Kill her, said the voice. *She is poisonous. You will never be happy until you are rid of her.*

A group of young men passed them. They were in high spirits and one of them winked at Dora as he strode by, making her trip in her embarrassment. Their voices seemed so loud in the relative stillness of the wood, but they were gone in an instant and silence was soon restored.

The path was steeper now. The trees had begun to thin out and the spaces between were bulging with moss-covered boulders. The route was now mostly on solid stone, the way worn smooth by countless shoes.

Not long now, said the voice. *It will soon be over.*

Dora's stepmother paused for a moment to adjust

her hat, and Dora soon caught up and stood along-side her. Her stepmother turned and smiled, and Dora hoped the smile she gave in return did not betray her true feelings, for she had never hated anyone so much as she hated this woman in that instant.

Look at her, said the voice. That smug grin. It has to end now. It has to!

Dora glanced at her father and he smiled back, evidently pleased to see the two of them standing so close. She felt her face flush at the words in her head. If he could only hear them, she thought, what would he think then?

It is perfect, said the voice. If done properly he will imagine himself to be a witness to an accident. But it needs to be quick. A swift shove and it's done.

Dora's stepmother was smiling at her again, but Dora could not hold her gaze. Instead she looked away into the woods and when she turned back her stepmother was standing on a rocky outcrop, looking out across the valley. Her father had walked on ahead a little way. They were nearing the summit now. Soon they would emerge from the cover of the woods.

A light breeze blew in from the north, carrying flecks of snow. They settled on Dora's hands and face and a shiver went through her body.

Now, said the voice. *While his back is turned and there is no one else to see. Now!*

Dora walked over to join her stepmother at the cliff's edge.

Now!

This was the moment. Dora felt almost as though she was standing to one side of herself, watching. Then she moved decisively, stepping back, and saw her stepmother lurching angrily towards the space she was vacating.

The look of fierce determination on her stepmother's face was replaced in an instant by wide-eyed terror as she clutched at the empty air ahead of her, realising too late that there was nothing, and nobody, to stop her falling headlong over the edge.

Dora's father turned at the sound of his wife's cry, just in time to see her tumble off the cliff and disappear into the valley below. There was a sickening thud as she hit a ledge and Dora saw her bounce like a doll to land far below in the branches of a tree. They found her resting there, head lolling at an impossible angle, snow settling on her pale blue eyes.

Dora had discovered a gift that day. She could

sometimes hold another person's thoughts in her head as though they were her own.

And this was only the start. She would discover that she could sometimes catch glimpses of distant events, or even the future, as though in a dream.

So Dora was shocked, but not surprised, when her father found yet another wife within a year. Luckily this one was far more to Dora's liking. She was quiet and kind, happy to share Dora's father and, as far as Dora could tell, utterly untroubled by murderous thoughts.

My stepmother finished her tale and looked at me with a twinkle in her eye that made me sure of the answer to the question I was about to ask.

'That was you in the story, wasn't it? You are Dora.'

'It is my middle name, it's true,' she said with a smile. 'But it is perhaps better if we talk of it only as a tale. After all, it is too fanciful to be real, is it not?'

Not long before, I would have agreed and discounted it as merely the meanderings of my stepmother's imagination. But I was wiser now.

My stepmother rose and walked slowly over to one of the large windows. It overlooked the terrace and offered a view past some shrubs, down the sloping lawn to the hedge that skirted along the lane running between the village and the church.

She seemed lost in thought and so absorbed that I got up from my chair and was about to leave the room when she spoke.

'There he goes again,' she said.

'Sorry?'

I received no reply and so I walked over to the window to stand alongside her. I could see that there was a boy of about my own age walking along the lane.

'His name is Edgar,' she said. 'I know his mother – a frightful woman. He's heading towards Pity's End.'

'Pity's End?'

'Yes,' my stepmother replied. 'It's on the other side of those woods over there. It used to be a school, you know. Your grandfather went there.'

I squinted into the distance. 'Was that the school where –'

'Yes,' she said, cutting me off. 'There was a terrible incident . . . Your grandfather has told you about it?'

'A little,' I said. 'But then, while I was on the train I saw . . . I dreamed . . . I felt as though I were there at the school. I imagined that I saw it all.'

The boy disappeared out of sight and I told my stepmother about my vision of the dormitory and of the bullying and of my grandfather's part in it. She sighed.

'Perhaps you have a gift yourself,' she said when I had finished.

I shook my head.

'I don't want to have one.'

My stepmother laughed.

'I'm afraid it is something that either you have or you do not have and there is nothing to be done but accept it, dear boy.'

I looked out of the window, thinking of the school and my grandfather. Snow was beginning to fall in fat, feathery flakes. A gust of wind spun the flakes into wild eddies until the garden was featureless, hidden behind a blur of whiteness.

'But is there a school there still?' I asked.

'Oh no,' said my stepmother. 'The headmaster had it converted back to a house many years ago, after parents took their children away from the school.'

'So does that boy – the boy we saw earlier – does

he live at the house?' I asked.

'Well, that's the strange thing,' my stepmother replied. 'I asked him where he was going once and he said he was visiting his Uncle Montague.'

'Montague?' I said. 'The same Montague who was headmaster? He still lives there, then?'

'That's just it,' she said. 'No one's lived there for years. Pity's End is quite ruinous.'

And the snow swirled around us with dizzying velocity. It felt as though we were inside a snow globe which had been lifted and shaken by some giant unseen hand.

The world without was white: as blank as a piece of paper on which the first words of a story were yet to be written . . .

© Judith Weik

Chris Priestley is the author of the chilling and brilliant *Tales of Terror* series and the haunting novel *The Dead of Winter*. He is also a talented artist. His illustrations and cartoons have been published in many national newspapers and magazines, including the *Independent* and the *Economist*. Chris lives in Cambridge, where he continues to write his seriously scary stories. To find out more about Chris, visit:
www.chrispriestley.blogspot.com